Pushpa M. Parmar is married with three children, living in Toronto, Canada. A Canadian of Indian descent, born in South Africa with a passion for history and 'herstory'. She has lived and worked in Canada, United States and the UK. Her father and family moved to Canada as political exiles from South Africa and were Anti-Apartheid activists in Canada.

2004.

Hope you enjoy
the book!

Love
Pushpa M. Parmar

P.S. Follow me on Instagram
and Facebook. And leave
a review on Amazon, Goodreads
or my social media!
xox

This book is dedicated to my mother and the many women who have no voice or 'herstory', lost and forgotten for their contribution to South African history. Thank you to my recently departed father who gave me the opportunity to live and learn as a Canadian and who was a model of being a 'good person and responsible global citizen'.

Pushpa M. Parmar

Promises for Tomorrow

Austin Macauley Publishers™
LONDON • CAMBRIDGE • NEW YORK • SHARJAH

Copyright © Pushpa M. Parmar 2023

All rights reserved. No part of this publication may be reproduced, distributed, or transmitted in any form or by any means, including photocopying, recording, or other electronic or mechanical methods, without the prior written permission of the publisher, except in the case of brief quotations embodied in critical reviews and certain other non-commercial uses permitted by copyright law. For permission requests, write to the publisher.

Any person who commits any unauthorised act in relation to this publication may be liable to criminal prosecution and civil claims for damages.

This is a work of fiction. Names, characters, businesses, places, events, locales, and incidents are either the products of the author's imagination or used in a fictitious manner. Any resemblance to actual persons, living or dead, or actual events is purely coincidental.

Ordering Information
Quantity sales: Special discounts are available on quantity purchases by corporations, associations, and others. For details, contact the publisher at the address below.

Publisher's Cataloguing-in-Publication data
Parmar, Pushpa M.
Promises for Tomorrow

ISBN 9798889108993 (Paperback)
ISBN 9798889109006 (Hardback)
ISBN 9798889109013 (ePub e-book)

Library of Congress Control Number: 2023903472

www.austinmacauley.com/us

First Published 2023
Austin Macauley Publishers LLC
40 Wall Street, 33rd Floor, Suite 3302
New York, NY 10005
USA

mail-usa@austinmacauley.com
+1 (646) 5125767

Thank you for the many Indian South African women who inspired me and provided their life stories as material and background for my book.

Cover illustration credit: Sabina Kim

Chapter 1

It was still dark in the early hours of the morning, in the summer month of December. Like most mornings, she woke to the birds singing their morning song, while they greedily ate the bread-crumbs she had left for them the night before. She often wondered what it would be like to be so free and happy all the time. Nothing else to do except look for food, find a mate, have babies and bask in the sun and play. Unfortunately, she was not a bird in this life but a young girl with nothing but work and responsibilities. Rekha turned over in the small bed, trying not to disturb her younger sister, Jyoti. Life would be very boring and miserable if she did not have someone to talk to. Rekha felt alone most of the time and Jyoti was the only one who could change that. She sighed and wished that just once they could sleep in. Just once, so Rekha could finish her wonderful dreams of eating all the sweets in the shop or running around outside with her friends and getting in trouble. Lately, she had been having dreams of a handsome man, tall with a kind face, who could take her away from her boring and uneventful life. She wished her life was like a story, like when the handsome Lord Shiva met the beautiful maiden Parvati, who was pious and faithful and served him unselfishly day and night. The story goes that one day, he took notice of her beauty and piety, fell in love with her and married her and they lived happily ever after…But that would never happen to her. What annoyed her the most was never being able to remember all her dreams, because they were always cut short by the morning sun. Rekha could feel the heat of the strong sunrays of summer, warming everything in its path. Also cut short by the never-failing rooster crows in addition to the chirping birds. They made such a racket. She tried to stay still with her eyes shut forcing her mind to recapture the lovely feeling of the dream she was having but it was useless. She finally gave up and lifted her tired head from the pillow and readied herself for the start of another boring day.

There was always something to do in this house. Today was Monday, she quickly realised, absolutely no time for dreams today. She rubbed the night's sleep from her eyes and tried to the see in her still dark room. A small amount of light that poked from under her door from the hallway gave her enough light to slowly focus on the dark wooden wardrobe which she shared with her sister, the straight back wooden chair next to it where her clothes lay which she wore yesterday and would wear today. There was not much in the room, there were no luxuries in this house. Rekha untangled herself from the sheets and her nightgown and swung her feet to the cold cement floor. As she stood, she heard the rooster crowing, signalling that she was late with her morning chores. Soon the whole household will be up and waiting for their breakfast. She must be quick or her mother would 'start' and then there would be no peace for a while. Rekha had the misfortune of being the firstborn girl, oldest at 12 years of age and was in charge of making the breakfast every morning. Ba had given birth to the fifth child who was now nine months ago, a baby girl Rita. She had two brothers, Jayesh, 11 and Arun, 10, both younger than herself by a year each and then Jyoti, nine, her younger sister who came after Arun. Ba had lost two babies before Rita. One baby boy was born too early and was stillborn, blue from being unable to breathe and then there was a tiny girl who managed to live only a few hours. Nobody talked about those babies. It was if they never existed. But everyone knew and felt the gap between the children. It was not normal, for most families, to have such a gap between babies. So, when Rita arrived and survived the first few days, she was greeted with relief and immense joy, especially from her parents who spoiled her, with as much attention as they could give. But truthfully, everyone spoiled her with attention. Even the boys talked to her when they came home from school. The boy's time, unlike the girls, in the family was precious and was metered out for specific activities. Their lives were divided into attending school, mealtimes, sleep time and a small amount of time reserved for schoolwork, a few hours on the weekend in the shop with their father and uncle and then the rest of their time was to be out and about gallivanting with friends in the neighbourhood.

As expected, most of the upbringing was left to Rekha and her mother, since the boys and Jyoti went to school. Rekha did not go anymore, it was decided a year before, just before Rita was born that Rekha was to stay home, too old at the age of eleven, for school and was needed to help out doing the housework and looking after the baby. But, Rekha was still sent to lessons early Sunday mornings, to learn how to read, write and speak Gujarati. All the children of all the Gujarati families in town had to attend. The lessons were broken in two levels, 'Beginners' for the very young and the 'Advanced level' for the older children where Jyoti and Rekha and their brothers were placed. Rekha loved school so much, not Gujarati school, which was mostly a chore and an unpleasant experience for most of the children. The teacher, Mrs Gopal, for the older or Advanced level, was very stern with the pupils and at times, bordered at mean. Most of the children did not like her and they all had agreed that she smelled of onions mixed in with bad body odour, evident with large wet underarm stains on her sari blouse. To add to the unpleasant experience, Miss Gopal was an unpleasant looking woman, short and rotund in figure with her huge nose and crooked teeth. She had the habit of spitting when she spoke, which usually landed on her unfortunate pupils. She always wore the same beige sari and put an excessively large chandla on her forehead. Some of the girls joked that she did that to prove that she was married, but who would marry her? By the end of the lesson, the prominent chandla would be smudged by her own hand, when she wiped the sweat from her brow. The small enclosed space used for the classes, had one small window that was too high to reach for her and to allow any fresh air in, so everyone suffered from the heat, but Mrs Gopal, most of all. They all tried, in vain, not to get too close to her or hoped she did not approach them. They really did not like any attention from her, because it meant she would offend them with her body odour or get a smack from the wooden ruler that she carried in her hand. At least one to two children were given a smack of the ruler on their hand or arm during lessons. This corporal punishment was Inflicted often if they did answer with the correct answer to the question she had posed or sometimes because they could not recite the verse, either correctly or not fast enough to her liking, that they were asked to memorise from week before. Most of the children stopped going to Gujarati school by the time they turned fourteen or fifteen years of age. Many of the poorer families could not afford to continue sending their children for long. Their children had to help out with earning money, in whatever way they could find, to support the family.

Rekha was not in that category, her family could afford both Gujarati school and regular school. Rekha missed the walks to and from school with her sister and the friends that joined on the way to school. She missed watching the daily hustle of life outside of her house. She missed saying hello to all the shopkeepers, as they opened every day, the smells of the bakery, the gathering of people at the Kafee. She especially missed talking and giggling with her girlfriends, in the common area of the school when they had break-time. Her best subject at school was Arithmetic and she had always received praise for her work and high marks on her tests from teachers. But not anymore, she had to learn to be a good cook and clean the house. According to her mother, school was a waste of time and Ba needed her help with the baby and the housework. How else was she going to be the perfect wife? Right now, she had to continue her *training* and make sure the family had their *nastoo* – breakfast.

Bapoojee would always need a good breakfast every day, because with his brother, Babookaka, they ran a successful variety shop-Poona Brothers Variety, read the big sign on the front of the shop. They sold some basics in men's clothing – hats, ties, socks, some fabric and sewing essentials, canned goods and the staples needed for any family, White or Indian. The family lived in the house connected to the back of the shops, in the Indian area of town, and the front door of the houses were located in the back. A wide dirt road separated the ten houses that faced each other, five on either side. This pattern of shops and houses stopped and started in groups of five, but continued for a good mile. There were all kinds of merchants in the Indian area; the tailors, the butchers, and fruit and vegetable shops who were their closest neighbours, literally next door. Further down the street, there was a bakery and dairy and a small shop that specialised in goods and clothes imported from India.

Babookaka and his wife, Bhartikaki, lived on the end of the same street as Rekha's family, about ten houses down, with his family. A swift walk would get Rekha there in 10 minutes. Babookaka lived behind a shop which he rented out from a muslim family. He had one girl and two boys, very small family by Indian standards, but his wife, Rekha's kaki was too ill after her last birth, so she could not have any more children. Babookaka was almost a clone of his brother, Rekha's father. But Babookaka was slightly smaller in frame and stature. He was always happy with a smile on his face and twinkle in his eye, a real charmer, people would call him. He was always telling jokes and stories, especially to the children. He had a way of keeping them very still and thrilled with a story of places and people, faraway and exotic. The children were always fascinated about the things *he knew and talked about.* But not many people knew, except the immediate family, how clever he really was. Babookaka was an avid reader and was more of an academic than a businessman. But there weren't many jobs for clever academic Indian men in Johannesburg. So, he was resigned to be happy and content to work with his brother in the shop. He was happily married to Bhartikaki, who was petite and slender like many Indian women. She had a nice enough figure and was a little more educated than the average woman. But Rekha thought she was more different than the other women she knew, especially different than her own mother. First of all, Bhartikaki beautiful eyes, with a mix of grey and green. Her hair was not long and straight like the hair in her family, but rather it was very curly and even when she pulled it back with a bun, it always escaped in curly tendrils and made a lovely frame for her heart shaped face. And the most beautiful thing about Bhartikaki was her gentle and kind heart. Rekha had never seen her aunt scold or shout at her children or give anyone a 'bad' face, which is what Rekha was used to seeing, from her own mother. Bhartikaki's children, Rekha's cousins were a few years older than the children in Rekha's family. Traditionally in Indian families, cousins were considered as close as brothers and sisters and addressed as such. The eldest daughter, Manjuben, who was considered ripe for marriage, as Rekha's mother always reminded her, at 16 years of age. The younger boys were twins, Naresh and Harish were the same age as Rekha. They all played together when they were younger, especially Rekha's brothers and Manjuben's brothers. Manjuben was the quiet older sister who had very little time to play with Rekha and Jyoti, but Rekha idolised her nonetheless.

Manjuben had a 'something' that was difficult to describe. It was not just her slender shape, with a small waist and slight curved hips and breast that were not too full and heavy, but just enough that always made her clothes look better than everyone else's. It did not matter what she wore, even a simple kitchen housecoat. She made it look better. Nor was it just her pretty face, her wide smile and green coloured almond-shaped eyes with long lashes. Nor was it her beautiful long black wavy tresses she kept braided in a single plait down her back that just barely reached her hips. It was more than her looks, she had some kind of magical aura around her. People were just polite and kinder with her in the room. She always had a smile on her face and was kind to everyone. She had a gentleness in her voice and in her mannerisms. Rekha sometimes fantasised that Manjuben was really a long-lost child of a movie star from Bombay or that her parents had adopted her and she was really a child from a *Maharaja's* family. Whenever she could, Rekha loved spending time with that whole family. She felt warm and safe in their presence and basked in the attention that Manjuben gave her when they were together. Rekha always wished that she could be as lovely and happy as Manjuben. But then, Rekha wished for a lot of things, things that would never happen in her family, no matter how wealthy and influential her family was. Things never changed in their lives, mostly because society made it that way and also because Rekha's mother would never change for anyone or anything, unless it benefitted her.

Chapter 2

The small town they lived in, Boksburg, was like other small towns of the Transvaal in South Africa. East of the largest city, Johannesburg, in the Union of South Africa. Babookaka always called it the "City of Gold" and told the children stories of how the streets were paved with gold. He said there were people from around the world who came here to build a fortune and get rich and it was the centre of South Africa and the richest city in Africa. He called it the 'land of opportunity' and that is why he and Bapoojee came from their small little village outside of Surat, Gujerat to be successful and rich. But everyone knew that the riches only belonged to the "Whites" of the country, who had all the advantages. The Indians had to make their own riches, from hard work and sacrifice, leaving their families behind wherever they came from and planted their roots in this dry, red earth in the Transvaal. There was, of course, the rich White area which included the main part of town, the surrounding houses and neighbourhoods were where all the Whites lived. Boksburg was not as rich as Johannesburg, but it was a rich White small town, busy with people coming and going. It had many kinds of industry, which included factories and near the outskirts of the city, a lot of mining sites and worker housing. All this industry and business created the need for markets and shops. Located on the outer edge of town, their street was one of the busiest streets in Boksburg. Everything that the Indians, or as the government labelled them – "Asiatics" of Boksburg – and inhabitants of smaller communities, needed could be bought on this particular street off Main Street. There was a shoe shop, a butcher shop where the Muslims could get their halal meat, and a bakery where they sold bread, buns and all the delicious biscuit and pastries that everyone enjoyed. The Whites came to shop in this area for one thing or another, but always in search of a good deal. Usually, they shopped exclusively in the White Areas, non-Whites were only allowed there with a good reason to be there and a *Passbook* for identification. Sometimes, the Blacks came to shop in Boksburg, but not too many, since they did not make enough money to shop in the Indian areas. Instead, they shopped at a small market at the main traffic junction in the middle of town or from the stalls set *up on the side of the roads*. Many of the new immigrants from India sold vegetables at their stalls, the Blacks bought the *mealies* or corn, as it was the mainstay of their diet. There was always one stall which sold roasted mealie *corn*, it was a nice snack for some, for others it was a meal. There were always the poorer Indian vendors who sold small items like thread, needles, cheap trinkets, chalk, chewing-gum, matches and cigarettes at the street junctions and the train stations. Rekha had not seen much of this because she, like her sister were confined to the house, school and the houses of their close friends and family. But they heard many of the stories her father and uncle told and from other visitors who would come from outside of their small town of Boksburg. After they did their duty of preparing and serving the *chaa* and savouries to visitors, they would sit in the kitchen and listen with great interest to every word the visitors spoke. They also wanted to go out into the big world and see it for themselves.

The rooster crowed again. Rekha grabbed and shook her sister's big toe.

"Quickly! The rooster has already crowed twice!" she announced to Jyoti, who always had trouble waking up in the morning.

She moved quickly through her bedroom door and down the hallway to the back of the house where the toilets were near the kitchen. It was still cold and her feet stung; in her hurried frenzy she had forgotten to put on her sandals, as she swiftly moved along the cold concrete to and from toilet. They were luckier than most, they had a sit-down toilet in the house. Most people they knew, had to use the outhouses set up in the alleys between the houses, others had squat-down toilets in their homes. These were basically, a hole in the ground, with two bricks for people to balance on while they relieved themselves. To flush, they had to pull a long chain from the chamber set up on the wall behind the hole. Rekha's family were extremely lucky and had both, the extravagant sit-down white toilet, like the Whites used, as well as, the kind where they had to squat down. The kitchen was also considered a large kitchen compared to other families' kitchens. Rekha's family spent a lot of time here, where they congregated for food, a good gossip or a good laugh, sometimes the occasional argument between siblings and husband and wife. Everything happened in the kitchen, good and bad. She washed her face and brushed her teeth in the bathroom connected to the kitchen which contained a small sink, mirror and shower stall, another thing that was considered a luxury by Indian standards in the small town. In the shower stall, there was a wooden stool and bucket that everyone used to bathe. The typical Indian bath, traditionally consisted of a bucket of hot or warm water, soap and a washcloth and smaller bucket or jug to rinse the body after soaping and scrubbing. Most squatted on their heels, while the elderly and very young used a stool to sit on while they bathed. The boys and Bapoojee always bathed first on alternate days before the girls, because they had to get ready for school and work. Rekha and her mother were usually the last to bathe in the house. The boys were always getting dirty and smelly, playing sports at school and playing with their friends outside, doing what young boys do. Rekha learned very early that the boys were special. More special and important than girls. The boys were not required to do much, except go to school and help out at the shop on the weekends and prepare to become income earners and manage their wives and families.

The morning rays shone bright and hot through the cotton netting kitchen curtains, hitting the table and floor with dancing patterns on the floor. It was going to be another dry, sunny day, with a slight breeze to ease the heat. But it was rare when the sun did not shine. Africa was always hot, winter and summer. Rekha opened the windows and let the heat of the morning sun and cool air into the kitchen. There was a soft breeze blowing the leaves on the trees. At least there will not be too much sand flying around today. Less sweeping for her to do and she didn't have much time today, she thought to herself. She went to the immense black coal stove on the other side of the kitchen, placed some coal and paper and kindling into the stove. She struck the match, threw it into the opening and stood there long enough to make sure it was lit. Moving as fast as she could, she filled a large pot of water to boil for the morning *chaa*, she raced back into her room changed into her daily clothes of a light-coloured grey cotton dress, plain in style. The dress had high rounded collar with short sleeves, with a thin band for the waist, not too tight and falling with an A-line skirt which stopped just above the calves. Her legs were bare and, on her feet, she wore simple brown sandals with a strap that separated her toes – *chappals* that were worn in the house while she completed her daily chores. These chappals, Rekha noticed, were beginning to fray and fall apart. For now, they would be fine but she would have to ask her mother for new pair soon, something she did not look forward to. She opened the door of her wardrobe, took out her comb and worked her hands through her hair releasing the knots, and plaiting her hair into two tight long braids down her back. She took a second to look into the small mirror on the inside of her wardrobe door. A round face with black almond shaped eyes looked back at her, she looked closely and realised that she had some grey colour in her eyes. There was a faint rim of grey that circled her pupils. Funny, she thought to herself, she had never noticed that before, but then Rekha never took too much time looking in the mirror. She never had the time. She did know that her nose was small and nicely shaped, a slight slope along the sides to a small round button tip. She only wished her teeth were a little bit straighter, having her top front teeth slanting inward. At twelve years of age, she was already a woman with small firm round breasts, with a deep curving of the hips, not all skinny and boyish like her younger sister. Her long jet-black hair was parted in the middle with two long tight braids. The plaits just reached past the middle of her back.

Rekha heard the morning wailings of the baby from the room at the end of the hallway.

"Rekha, bring me my *chaa*!" shouted her mother.

Oh no! Her mother was up and probably nursing the baby in bed and the chaa was not ready. She urged Jyoti to hurry, who was putting on her school uniform. Rekha prepared the toast, the chaa and set the table for the family. She took a small beaker filled with sweet milky masala chaa to her mother. The boys passed her in the hallway, busily tying on their school ties and tucking in white shirts for school, heading for the table she had set with food and chaa for them.

"Careful, don't make me spill it!" she warned them as they rushed past.

Rekha slowly opened the door with one hand and entered her parents' bedroom.

"What took you so long? Take these dirty nappies to the back for washing and bring me some fresh ones!" Ba ordered, "and don't forget to pick up everyone's clothes for washing today."

Rekha set the bekker on the small nightstand to her mother. And took a peek on at the baby who was drowsy and content nursing in her mother's arms.

"Bapoojee, your breakfast is ready," Rekha informed her father who was polishing his black shoes.

"Just now, let me finish cleaning my shoes. It would not be seemly for the boss to look shabby in front of the customers now, would it?" Her father grinned and gave her a wink.

"No, Bapoojee," Rekha answered with a broad smile, showing off her one dimple in her right cheek.

Rekha had a secret, one that she hadn't even shared with her sister. Everything else she told her sister, but not this. She loved her father the best. He was so kind, not just to Rekha, but everyone, the customers, the workers, his friends, his wife and especially children. And she truly believed that he loved her the most as well. As she revelled in this warm feeling, she took a moment and noticed that his hair was beginning to thin at the top of his head as he bent to tie the laces of his brown oxford shoes. He wore his white shirt and brown vest with matching trousers today. Bapoojee believed that you must always look your best, at all times and always wore shirt, tie and trousers. As he straightened, his pants looked a little tighter than usual and sat a little higher on his growing stomach. He must be eating too many chocolates at work again, she realised with a secret grin. Chocolates, of any kind, were his biggest weakness. He could never resist chocolates. And because all the children came to his shop to spend their savings on sweets and chocolates, he could never stop selling chocolates. Bapoojee was not handsome like in the films, but good-looking in an unconventional sense. He had a round face with heavy dark eyes and had a short thin moustache was very popular amongst Indian men, which was confirmed by the Indian films that came from India. When he wasn't smiling, he looked solemn and serious. But everyone knew that he had one of the kindest hearts. Rekha believed that he glowed as bright as the aura around Lord Krishna. She fantasised sometimes that her father was indeed the Lord Krishna, incarnated as her dear father, here to watch and protect her. He gave a wink again as he finished dressing, tucking his pocket-watch into his waistcoat. He was always giving her a wink or a smile when Ba was not looking.

"Go now, pour some *chaa* for your father, he cannot be late for work," Ba chided. Rekha's smile turned into a frown, but she turned away from her parents so they could not see her face. Her annoyance for her mother, whether shown by her face or her body, was unacceptable. Rekha moved quickly to the kitchen. That's all Ba could do…tell her to do this, do that. There was always something to do in this house. Rekha moved from room to room, picking up the dirty clothes left on the floor. She left the dirty clothes in the box on the kitchen floor to wash later. Rekha wondered for the hundredth time why they did not have maids like other families? They had money, they had a refrigerator, while lots of people used the old ice-box. They even had a car, one of those new black T-Ford models. No one else had a car, only those rich Whites! Bapoojee also had two good Black workers in the shop. Why would Ba not get at least get one maid to do the cleaning and the clothes washing? Rekha knew the answers to these questions, but would never say them out loud. Ba did not want to waste money on servants, why would she spend money when she had servants in the house already? Those servants were named Rekha and Jyoti.

It will be different when I get married, she promised herself, very different. Rekha promised herself many things for the future, but this promise remained the same, like a mantra she repeated to herself…She saw herself married to a handsome Gujarati with a broad forehead and dashing narrow moustache. He was to be an educated man who made enough money for a big house with maids and maybe a garden boy too, she would lounge around the house, planning meals for the evenings and having friends visit every day. Sometimes she and her handsome husband would go to *Bioscope* together and see the latest Hindi film. On Sundays, they would go to Zoo Lake and sit and have a picnic like all the other fashionable Indians of Johannesburg. It was *the* place to see and be seen. She would be dressed in the finest saris from India and she would be decked out in long gold earrings and a heavy gold chain and colourful matching glass bangles that would clink and tinkle on her wrists every time she moved. Her long black hair shining from luxurious oil treatments and put together in a fancy bun with flowers in her hair. Rekha had many fantasies like this, which she kept to herself. She did not want anyone laughing at her, even Jyoti, no matter how close they were and how much they shared with each other. Rekha knew that her dreams were something completely special to her, even though they may be outlandish and too improbable that she would ever be able to live the way the people lived in those Hindi films. But Rekha did not care. It made her feel better about her horrible life, working day in and day out.

Chapter 3

Rekha broke out of her daze, remembering that she had not had breakfast herself. Ba would bathe and then perform her daily morning *puja* at the small *mandir* in the corner of their front room and then be looking for her breakfast. Both the girls, from the time they were walking and talking had been brought up to pray like all good Hindu girls. When they started their "*monthlies*" or menstruations, they were told to fast on Tuesdays and Thursdays, for reasons they did not know at first. They also were told not to approach the *mandir* until they had finished their *monthlies.* At first, they had questions and wondered about all the rules and restrictions, but later learned and accepted that it was for their benefit to ensure they would get a husband and marry well. The fasting consisted of not eating meat and consuming fruit and milk all day and completing the process with performing a *puja* – prayers before eating a vegetarian meal. This fasting happened every week of their lives and like most rules and rituals that were handed down from their mother, it stayed with them and would always be a part of the lives.

Rekha's experience with her first bleed was at a very early age, just around her tenth year. She had been scrubbing the floor on her hands and knees when had felt a dampness between her legs and thought initially that she had slopped water on her dress while scrubbing. After she finished the floor, she got up and realised her dress was dry. She rushed to the toilet thinking she had soiled her underwear with urine. When she saw the smear of blood in her panties, she was horrified and scared. Her mind filled with questions but was too terrified to ask her mother. *What is this? Am I bleeding from inside? What if it doesn't stop? Will I die? I must speak to someone, but not Ba.* Rekha quickly got a fresh pair of panties and packed it with an old face washcloth, hoping it would stop the flow of blood or at least not leak too fast. She quickly washed the soiled panties in the bathroom, not wanting anyone to see what had happened and went outside to hang the panties to dry with the rest of the laundry she had put out earlier that morning. Later that day, before the children came back from school, Manjuben stopped by with some *achar* – pickled mangos her mother had made fresh that day. Rekha quietly beckoned Manjuben with her hand to come to her room. Rekha spoke with her head turned away in fear, unable to face Manjuben's reaction of horror on her face, once she explained to her cousin that she very ill from bleeding. Manjuben smiled at her with sympathy and explained what was happening to her was normal and expected and not to be afraid.

"Shame, you poor thing, this has happened very early for you. But don't worry. You will be fine. I will speak to your mother and she will take care of you." Manjuben did not say much more and left the room, leaving Rekha confused and shaking, but slightly relieved that she was not going to bleed to death. That evening Ba called Rekha into her room, making out she needed Rekha to help with the baby, but instead, gave Rekha some special rags, specifically made for the purpose for the *monthlies*.

"Now, this will happen every month and you better keep yourself clean. And remember, you must not touch the *diva* until you are finished. I will do the *diva* the days you are 'on'. And do not speak to anyone about this," Ba instructed without showing sympathy or any emotion. And that was that. Rekha did not completely understand still, but nodded and walked away, too afraid to ask any questions and put away her special rags. After that, it happened again each month, around the same time. She did not like it one bit. She thought it as a nuisance. Something else she had to worry about and add to her laundry load. Rekha soon realised that she was now a *'proper'* woman and that all women had the same thing and that they all carried on despite their *monthlies*, without any complaining and or talking about it. At those times of the month, Rekha would wish that she was a man and not a suffering woman. Men had it so easy.

Rekha quickly gathered her thoughts and realised that her milk was ready from the boiling. She added oats to make the porridge for her mother and herself. She also made a beaker of milky coffee, consisting of half milk and half coffee with lots of sugar and sat down alone at the kitchen table for a minute. Both she and her mother loved coffee and always had coffee after the morning tea. Rekha enjoyed this time, her favourite time of the day, the morning quiet, after the hustle and bustle of the family breakfast. She ate her porridge and drank her coffee in silence and recalled the events of this past Sunday. She wasn't sure what exactly had happened, but had a feeling that it was important, really important. It made her feel anxious, not knowing why she should feel that way. Remembering that day made her stomach knot, almost like she had eaten some bad food. She would have to ask her father when he was not too busy or tired. Maybe she could ask him just before supper, while he was enjoying his whiskey in the front room.

Rekha remembered how strange Ba had acted on the Saturday before. As soon as the breakfast had finished, Ba had instructed her and Jyoti to clean the front room from top to bottom. This was not unusual since every Saturday was cleaning day anyway. Ba had also scrubbed the cement floor and then waxed and polished until it gleamed into the night. As usual, the little *mandir* praying area that every Hindu home kept, had to be cleaned. Inside the *mandir*, there was small statues of the gods – Shiva, Ganesh and a photo of Krishna. There was a small brass cup on a brass pedestal where the *diva-lit flame* was placed and used. A small potato was used to hold the incense that was lit every day. Jyoti swept the front room and the fancy rug with the red and pink bright flowers with broom in hand and then she cleaned the glass cabinets and the few picture frames of various gods and goddesses on the walls. She used vinegar and old newsprint to clean the glass cabinets. Ba was extra fussy about the chesterfield being too dusty and making sure the doilies, placed on the chesterfield as decoration, were bleached and washed to be extra white.

"I want everything to be right, just right for the visitors tomorrow, girls make sure that everything is just right," Ba kept saying all day. She did not look or sound normal that day, muttering to herself all day, while checking every little detail twice.

The girls had stopping listening to her hours ago and continued with their chores. Ba stood in the front room and counted the glasses, plates and teacups she reserved to use for special visitors. Rekha had not seen her mother this nervous about visitors before. Rekha watched her mother walk quickly to and from the kitchen, making her cotton pale blue sari swish with each step. Her thin arms moving at a frantic rate, her thin fingers touching this and that, her long black plait swaying back and forth at her back with her non-stop movements. She was a petite woman, barely reaching a full five feet tall, she was always surprised Rekha with the amount of strength and energy she could muster when necessary. Rekha heard other people compliment her father on how pretty his wife was. They admired her large eyes, small nose and high cheek bones, heart-shaped face and long straight black hair and her light complexion was always commented on by people. No matter how many children her mother had, she maintained her young girlish figure. But Rekha did not see what other people saw. Rekha saw a mean-spirited, controlling woman and who never had a good thing to say or do for her daughters. Ba would croon and caress her sons, who would melt at her touch and with her husband, she was the quiet and obedient wife. She was the perfect Indian mother and wife to the world. Rekha could never see her mother the way other people saw her. She only saw and experienced cruelty and because of that, did not see a beautiful woman but rather an ugly person, almost like a rabid dog at times. But this was never discussed or voiced out loud. To speak badly of parents and elders was unacceptable and disgraceful.

Rekha and Jyoti still wondered who were these people coming to visit? These 'special' visitors as Ba called them. Then after lunch, it was time to bake for the week. Usually, they baked sugar biscuits, jam tarts and plain yellow cake for the family to have with their chaa in the afternoon. Ba would occasionally request that a special pastry, such as *gulab jamuns, naan katai or kooksiesters* be made for visitors who always came on Sunday afternoons. Ba wanted *koeksisters* this day, enough for two families. The girls worked swiftly, but carefully, so as not to burn themselves with the hot oil used for the frying the small log shaped donuts, which were then dropped into a hot pot of sugar syrup. Jyoti's favourite part was to roll the sticky hot donuts into shredded white coconut. When the mother wasn't watching, the girls would eat the coconut that kept falling off the *kooksiesters* or dip their fingers into the hot syrup. The smell of the rose water in the syrup and the cardamon and coconut brought the boys out of the shop, where they worked on Saturdays, they gobbled up a couple *kooksiesters* each. Ba was counting the sweet donuts to make sure there was enough for the visitors, but her boys could have as much as their stomachs could hold.

"Eat, eat my boys, so you can be big and strong," Ba crooned.

It was good to be a boy, they ate everything, they went to school and they got to work and be out in the world. *I hope God makes me a boy in my next life,* Rekha wished to herself, this wishing which happened almost every day of her life.

Throughout the day, Rekha and her sister kept looking at each other quizzically, questioning Ba's anxious behaviour that day, but not being brave enough to voice it. They could never and would never voice complaints or questions about Ba. If by chance they were caught whispering, they would both get what Ba like to call a '*good hiding*' which consisting of a few smacks by her hand or whatever convenient weapon she could find. Rekha wondered many times what a *'bad hiding'* was compared to a '*good hiding*'? Ba liked to use the *velan* – a thin wooden rolling pin that was used to make *roti*-thin flat bread made from flour and hot water, or sometimes the broom, but the *velan* hurt the most because it was so thin and hard. At times, her rage was uncontrollable and she would pick up anything that was handy. Rekha remembered when she had opened her mouth that one time with a sarcastic remark without thinking and was rewarded with a smack at the back of her head with a cooking pot. Luckily, the pot had been empty. Rekha had egg sized bump and a bad headache for days. The girls learned very early in life, to keep their mouths shut, only in the darkness of night and in the privacy of their room, did they whisper or gossip of the things that happened that day. If they could not contain themselves, and had the burning need to complain or question things, they would meet behind the outhouse, always checking first to see if anyone was using the outhouse. Finally, the baking for the visitors was done, Ba used the large tin biscuit containers to store the sweet pastries, biscuits and cakes and put them on the top shelf of the cupboards in the kitchen. It was understood by all that no one was allowed to touch them, not until the visitors would have their fill and had left the house. After eating supper and washing up, the girls were tired but satisfied from the day's work.. They went to their room, wasting no time, they changed, brushed out their hair and slid into the bed they shared. They lay face to face and whispered about why Ba was so nervous, guessing who these visitors could be and finally after many guesses and giggles, they drifted off to sleep, dreaming of eating biscuits and *kooksiesters* to their heart's content. *Tomorrow would come soon enough and then they would know...*

Chapter 4

Sunday came quickly and both girls were out of their bed before the crow could sing his crooked song. The shop was open for half a day. Bapoojee said the Whites didn't believe in work on Sunday, their God did not allow work. It was the Whites' day for prayer and rest. So business was a little slower than usual. The Muslims and Hindus took this day as a social day and spent it outside, visiting or having a picnic or going for drives and a little shopping. Rekha had made breakfast of toast and tea for everyone, as usual, and was clearing up the table with Jyoti.

"Rekha, come here my girl," beckoned Ba from her room.

Rekha quickly went to see what needed to be done. Ba was putting the baby down for her morning nap. She turned to Rekha, grabbed her arm in a tight grip.

"Now listen to me carefully, I don't want any of your nonsense today, you will behave and do as your father and I tell you," warned Ba.

"Jee, Ba, I will behave," Rekha meekly replied.

"Also you must wash your face, put on your nice dress, your nice ribbons and your fancy white socks and take this eye *kohl* and put some on," she added, as she handed her the eye makeup stick.

"Quickly go now and get ready! And remember, no nonsense!"

"Jee Ba," Rekha, now excited, took the *kohl* and hurried to her room to get ready. Something was really wrong with Ba today? Rekha was never allowed to put on *kohl*. She looked at herself in the small mirror? Did she look dirty? She washed quickly and changed into her one and only nice dress. It was white with small yellow flowers embroidered on the lapels and the hem. She had only worn it once before, for a wedding a few months ago. Her socks were also practically new. She polished and buffed her black shoes, trying in vain to put some shine into them. She finally had to rub some Vaseline into them for the shine she was looking for. She was fixing her hair into tight plaits when her sister walked in the room.

"What did Ba want? And why are you putting your nice things on? Why am I not allowed to put my nice things on?" Jyoti asked as she helped finish plait Rekha's hair.

"Ba told me to put them on. And then, she gave the *kohl* to put on my eyes!" she confessed with quiet delight.

"Quickly, you put some on too, she won't notice. She is too nervous and busy." Rekha urged.

The sisters got ready and appraised each other with a huge grin, thinking how pretty and grown-up they looked. Rekha looked at her reflection and noticed that the kohl made her eyes more grey than black. She bit her lips to make them a little rosy. The white dress and white ribbons made her olive skin shine. What was she doing? She questioned herself. All the cleaning and preparation and Ba's nervousness made her totally out of sorts, but in a good way. It almost felt like there was a family wedding happening.

Voices floated from the front room. Rekha could hear her father welcoming the visitors.

Oh my, they were here already! She and Jyoti rushed to the kitchen to make sure the tea was boiling; the food was set on their best trays and the teacups and saucers were set out.

"Rekha, my girl, bring *pani* for our visitors," called Ba from front room.

Rekha poured cold water kept in the refrigerator, into small glasses already set on the tray. She lifted the tray, praying she would not drop it. She took great care and kept her eyes on the tray, as she entered the room. She walked gingerly over to the first person to offer water. She lifted her eyes and immediately recognised the man sitting in front of her. "Thank you, my child," the uncle said with a huge grin.

His round face split in half when he smiled. His heavy and thick fingers took the glass gingerly as she was offering something precious and fragile. He reminded her of the God Ganesh, with his bulky build, which barely fit on the small chesterfield where he sat next to her Bapoojee. Rekha could not help it and grinned back at him, revealing her dimples. She offered the tray to the wife, sitting on a chair, next to him.

This *auntie* was a handsome woman, with a high forehead and a long narrow nose. But she did not seem too friendly today, she gave a look that scared Rekha a little. The auntie had henna tattoo dots on her face, one on her chin and the other between her cheek and nose. Not many women had those permanent henna tattoos. And her *chandla* was so big! *Did she use nail varnish or lipstick for the chandla?* She also wore a fancy green silk sari with a beige gossamer border. Rekha went from person to person, serving them water and realised that she knew all these visitors. Why didn't Ba just tell her who was coming? This family came to visit all the time. Bapoojee played cards and had drinking sessions with this uncle, at least once a month. They owned and ran a small dairy shop on Marshall Street in Johannesburg. The big city she had hoped to visit one day. She greeted the eldest daughter who was recently married, in the last few months, she was around the same age as her cousin, Manjuben, and was very friendly. There were two girls younger than her, very chatty too. They sat whispering and giggling to each other, while the adults chatted. And then another older couple, whom she faintly remembered seeing at a wedding or two, she assumed they were related to this family in some way. The older couple had driven the visitors to the house.

She tried not to rush and tried, in vain, not to show her surprise and annoyance at her mother for not telling her anything. She finally stopped at the last person sitting in the corner, a young boy, maybe a couple of years older than her, she knew this boy but only as a member of this family, his face not familiar at all. In Rekha's family, as in many Indian families, young girls did not look at boys, they did not talk to boys and they certainly did not smile at boys. This boy looked very nervous and uncomfortable. His hazel eyes were darting from wall to wall, as if he was looking for an escape route, as if a fire would break out any time soon. He was smartly dressed, in white shirt and grey trousers. But his trousers were too short and tight for him. Most probably, passed down from an older family member. He looked very uncomfortable in his clothes, occasionally pulling at his collar and tugging at his trousers. His short wavy black hair was oiled and neatly combed. His face was nice, with his chin ending in a sharp point. He kept his eyes down as she approached and kept looking down and she then noticed that he had a nose just like his mother. Funny, Rekha thought to herself, the kitchen is always the hottest room in the house, but he was sweating and wiping his hands and forehead with his cotton handkerchief in his hand. At times, he looked like he was trying to strangle the poor *hankie*. He took the glass without a smile and gulped it in one swallow. No polite sips for him, as was required of visitors when offered any refreshment. Rekha finished offering water and reminded herself to walk back slowly back to the kitchen, she remembered that Ba hated it when she darted from room to room.

"You will never guess who the visitors are!" Rekha challenged Jyoti, whose eyes were as big as saucers.

"I don't know, just tell me." Jyoti was eager to know. Rekha grinned at her in silence, enjoying torturing her sibling for a moment.

"Come now, don't be like that," whined Jyoti.

"Okay, okay, the visitors are the dairy shop people!" Rekha confessed finally.

"The Lala's, but they're not special, we see them all the time!" she whined, "We did all this work for them!?"

"Yes, that is exactly what I was thinking," replied Rekha. "They have their fancy clothes on too! Like they just came from a wedding."

"Rekha, where are you? Come now and sit with us," Ba beckoned Rekha. Both girls looked at each other with shocked faces. They had never heard their mother use such a sweet tone to her voice when she spoke to the girls. Clearly, she was *putting it on* for the visitors and they were surprised and shook their heads in wonder. *Since when do they sit with visitors?* Only the boys were allowed. Rekha walked backward slowly toward the room, shrugging her shoulders and making a face of wonder at her sister, desperately trying to figure out what was going on. At the door, she turned slowly and entered the room. She felt nervous, the butterflies in her stomach were now doing big somersaults. She was thankful she had not eaten too much this morning. She hesitated at the doorway, wondering what she was needed for now. Her father beckoned to sit next to him. She quickly moved toward her father and squeezed herself into the small opening between her father and Mr Lala. She felt safer as she pressed sideways into his arm and felt his body heat and then wondered why she needed to feel safe.

"No *dikri*, you must come sit with Bharat, here is a chair for you," motioned Ba.

Rekha froze for a second, she just stared at her mother. Ba was pointing to the chair next to Bharat, but this seat was fine. She felt Bapoojee's hands grabbing her arms and gently but firmly pulling her to her feet and gave her a nudge toward the waiting chair. She felt all the eyes of the room on her as she moved her heavy feet toward the chair. She quickly sat down and felt the hard wood of the chair under her. She looked at her feet and saw Bharat's black shoes, in her line of vision. Funny, she thought, his shoes were scuffed and dusty at the toes, he looked so clean and neat at first glance. Maybe his family had to drag him here, forcibly by the arms, while his feet scraped the ground! She quickly glanced sideways at him and saw that his eyes were firmly planted on his shoes as well. She felt a pang of sympathy for him for a moment. *Was he just shy? Maybe he knew what was going on?* That would explain why he looked so nervous. Rekha remained silent and motionless, partly because she remembered her mother's warning earlier that morning, and partly out of fear of the unknown. For the next ten minutes, things were a blur, hands moving, people talking, smiling and laughing. She felt like she was in a dream, but not a good dream, rather a strange dream. Food was being put into her mouth, she obediently opened her mouth and ate it, she tasted sweet dry paste. Her hands felt heavy with something like a large rock. People were touching her face. Her head was feeling heavy and hot. Did she have a fever? She blinked and focused on her hands and realised she was cradling a coconut with some money in her hands. She quickly darted her eyes to Bharat. He was also holding a coconut and money in his hands. The seconds and minutes dragged slowly, the two of them sat in silence, not moving, intently inspecting the hard and hairy fruits that weighed heavily in their hands and on their minds.

Chaa was being served, the trays of biscuits and *gulab jamuns* were on the small oval coffee table. The chatter of happiness and excitement surrounded them, the clinking of tea cups on saucers interrupted by the chatter. Rekha thought she should be in the kitchen with her sister and helping with the serving. But her body remained glued to the chair. She heard murmurings…"such a nice girl"… "handsome couple one day"…"the promise is fulfilled now." Rekha tried to make sense of the conversation, but her head was swirling and she could not make her brain work. Then she heard something she recognised and understood…

"Rekha, go help your sister in the kitchen," Ba asked gently.

Rekha popped out of her chair without a word, not a good-bye, not a glance back at the boy and the visitors, and swiftly walked back to the kitchen. Jyoti's anxious face greeted her with a million questions.

"What happened? Why do you have *chandla* on your forehead? Oh, you have money and a coconut in your hands! Did I miss something?" she asked as she surveyed her sister from head to toe, breathless at the end.

Rekha dropped the money and coconut onto the table as if they would burn her hands. She put her head in her hands and shook her head. She felt something on her forehead, something powdery and hard. She rubbed her forehead, and looked at her hand. *Was it blood? No, it can't be!* It was *kunkoo* with grains of white rice, used in religious ceremonies for blessing. *How did that get there?* She vaguely remembered someone touching her forehead, or was it more than one person?

"Rekha, why do you have a *chandla* on your forehead?" she questioned again.

Rekha could see that Jyoti was very anxious, mostly about the fact that she had been left out of something, but not knowing what exactly, but definitely something.

"Tell me what happened!" she demanded.

"I don't know," Rekha finally answered. "I remember sitting next to Bapoojee and then he moved me to a chair and then Ba was telling me to help you in the kitchen."

"Did anyone say anything to you?" she asked.

"No, no, nothing."

"Oh, I hear them leaving, come help me collect the dishes and food." Jyoti rushed to the front room.

The visitors and Bapoojee were standing on the *stoep*, saying their goodbyes and thank-yous. Ba went to her room to check on the baby who would surely be hungry soon. Bapoojee stood at the door and waving and smiling until they were out of sight. Rekha could hear the sounds of car doors shutting and finally the engine noise fading away.

"I want the food put away and dishes washed and dried before I come back to cook the supper," Ba barked sharply, as she returned.

Rekha was still in a slight fog, the dishes rattled in her hands, as she cleared up the coffee table.

"Jee, Ba," she replied as calmly as she could.

She did not look at her mother and hid her face. She felt manipulated, with Ba pulling her strings like a puppet in a show. The girls got their chores done as swiftly as possible. They did not want to get in their mother's way when she came back and they were desperate to talk about what had just happened. They agreed, through whispers, to meet behind the outhouse, they could not wait for nightfall. While washing the dishes, Rekha rubbed her forehead with the back of hand and was shocked again to see the red of the powder. She vigorously rubbed and splashed cold water on her face to remove all traces of the powder, and any reminders of today. A light touch on her shoulder made her jump.

"You are a good daughter, Rekha," Bapoojee said as he cupped her face in his hand and rubbed her cheek.

He was smiling like he always smiled with his mouth, but this time, his eyes weren't smiling. The softness and his voice and hand made Rekha heart tighten. She felt the rush of heat in her head and water pooling in her eyes. The slap of Ba's champals on the concrete floor, broke the moment. Bapoojee quietly walked away, mumbling of checking something in the stockroom. Rekha kept her eyes down and finished washing and drying the dishes. When she finished, she glanced at the table and noticed that the money and coconut was missing. *Did Ba take them? What should she do? Ask or pretend that she never saw the money?*

"Rekha, peel some potatoes and Jyoti, you clean and wash the rice," Ba instructed.

Rekha was thankful, she didn't have to do the rice, she disliked having to search for bugs and pebbles in the rice. Peeling, washing and dicing the potatoes took no time at all. Ba set two pots of water to boil, one for the rice and one for the lentils to make *dahl*. Then she set a large frying pan on the black stove, poured some *ghee* to heat up and then tossed in the spices to cook the potatoes. Rice and *masoor dahl* with *potato fry* was a favourite in this house. The kitchen was heating up with steam from water boiling and oil being used to cook. The pungent aroma of turmeric, cayenne pepper, ginger and garlic were wafting through the house, finding every nook it could. Indian food aromas had a habit of touching and clinging onto everything in the house, furniture and clothes. Every day, Rekha knew what the neighbours were cooking just by the smell. Ba opened the windows to ease the stifling heat. She wiped the sweat on the back of her neck.

"Go, check on the little one, Jyoti," Ba said as she finished cooking the supper.

Rekha went to use the toilet, while Jyoti did as she was told, both grateful for the break from kitchen work. Rekha finished washing her hands and then waited patiently for Jyoti behind the outhouse.

Rekha squatted on her heels and played in the sand with her fingers. She started to draw abstract patterns and realised that she had drawn the shape of a coconut and also a face, Bharat's face. Embarrassed, she erased the drawings with the palm of her hand, wishing she could erase the Whole episode of this morning—just like that! Life could be so easy if we could just erase parts of our lives with the wave of one hand. *But even the God and Goddesses did not have the power, they had to live with consequences of their actions. Then how could she, a mere mortal, possibly do that?* Her thoughts were abruptly interrupted by Jyoti, who arrived breathless, from rushing in fear of being caught.

"What happened? What did they say, why did they come?" She fired off questions still unanswered, "why did Ba make such a fuss over them? They were not special! We see them all the time!"

"I am not really sure," Rekha answered, nervously looking over her shoulder. "I remember sitting down next to Bapoojee and then I ended sitting next to Bharat and then it is difficult to remember what happened after that." She slowly told little details about the boy and bits of conversation that she could remember. She was too embarrassed, even to tell her only confidante, how terrified she was and how she remained frozen in one position with her eyes on the floor.

"Do you think they will come back again?"

"I don't think so," Rekha reassured her sister with more confidence than she really had. Inwardly, she prayed to Krishna and all the other Gods she could think of that they did not return and she did not have to go through this again. Suddenly, she felt a sharp pain at the back of her head and was thrown back onto her backside. "Ahhhh," she shrieked. Ba had a firm grip on one of her plaits and was pulling. Then she reached across for Jyoti and had both of them by the plaits, dragging both of them into the kitchen.

"What is this?" she demanded, "I turn my back for one minute and what do I find? Two useless, lazy girls *skinnering*...about God knows what!? When there is work to be done. God did not give me five arms and five legs to do the work. No...instead, He made me an Indian woman with two useless daughters! If I was a man or a Whitie, then my life would so *lekker*! No babies, no cooking, no cleaning, no silly children needing eating up my head every time I look!" She pushed them into the corner of the kitchen as she lectured them and pulled out the *velan* from the drawer and began hitting them. She did not aim for their backsides. She let that rolling stick land wherever it wanted. On their heads, their legs, their backs. They cowered together with their arms up, protecting their faces. They tried to muffle their screams and shrieks of pain, not giving her the satisfaction, of knowing how much pain she was inflicting. Only, their tears betrayed them, flowing down their cheeks and landed on their bodies like a fountain of shame and hate. Hate for the person who was inflicting this pain and shame for feeling this way about her mother. *Is this how all mothers treated their daughters? A mother must truly hate her children to treat them this way, but did it not create hatefulness in return? How could they ever get away from this misery and pain?* Then Rekha remembered what all Indian children are taught, to be respectable and dutiful to their parents all their lives. *There must be some way to get away.* Rekha wondered with tears rolling down her face. The tears only angered their mother more.

"What are you crying for?" she shouted, "I should be the one crying. I come to this Africa and all I do is make babies and work like a dog! I will give you something to cry for!" throwing her weapon wildly at them. Once again, Rekha was shocked and terrified at the strength that came from this small woman.

"Stop it! Stop this nonsense right now!" her father's voice boomed. The blows suddenly stopped, but the sting lingered. Not knowing, there at the moment, that the pain would linger in her mind and her heart much more than on her body. Rekha looked up at her father, who had now taken the *velan* from her mother and spoke in voice that sounded calm, but was clearly strained. He was trying to control his anger.

"Why must you do this? Is it not enough to know that they will leave this house one day? And we don't know if these people will shout them or beat them. No matter what promises they make to us. Stop this and let them have some peace and happiness," He pleaded with her, but it did seem to make much difference. Ba looked at the girls huddled together, wiping their tears and snot from their faces. She looked back at her husband. He looked at the girls and shook his head, not being able to understand why this wife and mother was so cruel to her own children. He could not understand, but neither could she. She did not even realise that she treated the girls differently to the boys and what those reasons were. To her, the girls represented something she could not talk about or explain. She like most of them, did not have the understanding that she controlled her ego and basic emotions, within the boundaries of the rule of men, to guide her through life. Fulfilling her duties as a wife and mother was first on her list of priorities. But then she, like most people, had the ever-hungry ego that needed feeding and controlled every part of her life, leaving no room for reason. Her ego guided with pure emotions – good and bad and then those actions or reaction to those emotions. She yearned for what they, her girls, did not even know they could have. A possibility that they had a better life or would have a better future. She resented the girls for it, for something she could not convey or understand. So, their relationship would always be like this. A constant tug of war of control and hope between the mother and daughters.

She glared at the girls, as if to say "this was not over!" and walked away with her nose in the air to her bedroom. The slapping of her champals on the concrete faded away, until they heard the door creak open and shut with a slam.

The girls finished cooking the supper and set the table. Ba walked out of her room, greeted the boys and sat at the table, as the boys came in one by one, after playing and roaming around with their friends. She gently reprimanded them to wash their hands before sitting down, while they joked and giggled with each other about what they had done, teasing each other their antics in the neighbourhood. They were too distracted with their own happiness to notice the stony silence around them. There was no other conversation from the parents, except for the occasional request for a dish from Bapoojee. Rekha and Jyoti kept their eyes on their plates her food and ate quietly. They did not want provoke their mother further. After the meal was done, the girls cleared up, washed and dried the dishes and went to their room. They were tired from all the cleaning and cooking and now their bodies were sore from the beating. Rekha felt like she could sleep for days, her mind felt foggy, like a spider had crawled into her brain and spun a spider-web. She moved without thinking, doing things by habit, she washed her face and combed out her plaits, put on her nightgown. There was no chatter and gossip tonight, too tired and too terrified of their mother hearing them. As the girls got into their bed, they were surprised to see two chocolate bars, one for each of them, on their pillows. They did not speak, but allowed themselves a small smile. They knew that Bapoojee had left the treats for them, out of sympathy that he could never show in front of his wife. Jyoti ripped the wrapping off and ate hers quickly. Licking her fingers to make sure she got every last bit and also to make sure that none got on the bed or on their night clothes. She got into bed and slept straight away as if the chocolate had been a sleeping drug. As the sleep took hold of her head and her eyes grew heavy… Rekha promised herself that when she had a family that she would never to do this to her children. *She would never beat her children. No matter how naughty they were. Never!*

Chapter 5

Rekha was still mulling over the events of the weekend on Monday morning, as she finished off her breakfast of porridge and milky coffee. She must find the right time to speak to her father. She had to find out what had happened, she was desperate to know. He had to explain his words to Ba, after he had stopped the beating. *Were she and her sister going somewhere? Being sent off to work in someone's house? Was Ba trying to get rid of them?* What had happened to the money and coconut that had sat in her hands for what seemed eternity. It was like nothing had happened at all. But she had the bruises on her body, a clear reminder of what yesterday. Rekha suddenly realised that she was not alone and Ba had walked in the kitchen, poured herself some sweet milky coffee from the bekker warming on the black stove and sat to eat her porridge. Rekha quickly jumped and went to the basin to wash up the morning breakfast dishes. She could not look at mother, she did not want her mother to see the heat of anger in her face, afraid she would get another beating. Rekha stood with her back strong and straight, but as she washed, she could see the numerous bruises on her arms that had turned black and purple. Her legs began to shake a little and some tears managed to escape before she could stop them. She silently prayed to Lord Shiva needing his power to sustain her and give her strength. She managed to pull herself together and finished washing and drying the dishes. She must not fall apart, not with her watching!

Rekha fetched the dirty laundry and took it outside to the back of the house. She used the strong-smelling laundry soap bar rubbing all the stains and dirt off each item of clothes. She made sure she inspected each piece of clothing for anything she might have missed. Rekha had heard some rumours of women who ate the soap, in a desperate attempt to kill themselves. She wondered if she would ever consider that option. But why should she? She knew that one day, she would marry and leave this house forever. Leaving her father would be the hardest part, but that is the way life was. One day, her parents would not be her parents, they would be replaced by her husband's parents. Her husband and his family would 'own' her. She relived her fantasy of a handsome rich man saving her from this drudgery. But right now, she had more important things on her mind. First, she had to rinse these clothes, ring them out and hang them on the clothesline and then go back into the kitchen.

When she walked into the kitchen, Babookaka was sitting at the kitchen table enjoying a cup of *masala chai*, she had left on the stove to keep warm. She liked him so much, he was nice like Bapoojee, but funnier. Rekha loved listening to his stories of India, the Gods and Goddesses and sometimes, when he had too much *'tot'* – *drink.* he would imitate the shop customers in silly voices.

"Well, look at this girl here, sorry…I mean madam now, *howzit*?" he asked through a smile and a mouthful of *kooksiesters* left over from the other day, not hesitating to reach for another to soak in his tea before eating it, happily munching on the tea-soaked donut.

"I am fine Babookaka, how are you today?" she couldn't help grinning, like her father, he had a sweet-tooth and could not resist sugar of any kind.

"Good, but you know how these bunions are always giving a trouble…I am taking a rest right now, the shop is quiet." He stuffed more coconut covered donuts into his mouth and slurped his *Chai* from the saucer.

She looked around for her mother and guessed that she was in the bedroom looking after the baby. Maybe, he knew something…then she would not have to bother her father.

"I heard you had some very special visitors yesterday." He grinned and wiggled his eyebrows at her.

He knew! She looked around the room and listened for footsteps coming from the bedroom. She could hear a faint murmur from her mother's bedroom. She must be talking to the baby again.

"But Kaka, please, you must help me…tell what you know!" she pleaded.

About what, my *poppet*?"

"The visitors, why did they come? And Ba made such a fuss, and then they gave a coconut and some money and now it is missing! What should I do?" She fired at him with fearful eyes, looking out for her mother.

"They did not tell you? That is lousy," he asked in surprise.

"No, no, they told me nothing. Ba told me to behave and sit and be quiet."

He remained silent for a minute, deciding whether to tell Rekha or not. If they found out that he had told her, they will accuse him of interfering. But he cared this little girl like she was his own. He could not leave her in the dark.

"My girl..." he paused, flicked his eyes around the room, looking for unwelcome ears, "they have promised you to that boy."

"No," the heat started from the top of her head and moved down to her stomach. She stood but her legs were verging on collapse.

"To...to...Bharat?" she sputtered, gripping the back of the chair for support. Her uncle nodded. Rekha stood immobile as a flood of emotions passed from brain to her heart and coursed through her body. Shock came first, how could they do this with her knowing? Then anger, they have given me away to them!? Then shame, how could she have not known, the ceremony, her dressing-up, the kohl, the boy, her mother acting strangely. Then finally, a small flame of happiness was lit and it grew until she thought she would burst...maybe, just maybe this will be her way out, finally, someone has listened to her prayers! Was it Krishna, Shiva, Ganesh? Right now, she did not care, at least someone has answered her prayers. She had to give thanks when she did her *puja*.

"Rekha? *Poppet*? Are you okay?" Her uncle's voice brought her out of her daze.

"Jee Kaka, everything is fine, everything is perfect," she whispered.

He seemed content with her answer, finished his chaa and went back to the shop.

But she had so many questions! When would she get married? Where would she live? Would he be a good husband, as she had dreamed a million times? She felt dizzy with happiness, her feet hardly touching the floor. Through the day, her happiness showed in small ways, her back straight with head higher, she moved a little faster and she did not think once about the amount of work that Ba gave to her. She was content and now, she had hope. Hope for a life with freedom, with a man of her dreams to do as she pleased. She made tea, set the plates and warmed yesterday's leftovers for lunch and waited. She waited for her sister to come home from school to tell her the joyous news. *She would finally be leaving this house one day!*

When Rekha first broke the news to Jyoti, she reacted with shock and surprise. But that soon turned into sadness and she was inconsolable for days. Jyoti did not look forward to the day she too would be taken out of school to work in the house. She would be alone. Jyoti did not stop to think that Rekha was all alone for these past years. Jyoti sulked for days not wanting to discuss it. Eventually, the silence turned into denial and she pretended like nothing had happened at all. Rekha was in despair over her sister's reaction. She was rejected every time she attempted to speak to Jyoti about her engagement. After a few days, she just gave up. *How could Jyoti be so selfish? This was my only chance of happiness and she was only thinking of herself!* Rekha finally decided that she did not need her. Night after night, they went to bed in silence, their backs to each other, trying in vain, not to touch each other in the narrow bed. Weeks went by before life continued as it was before the engagement. She cooked, cleaned and helped Ba with baby, while her siblings went to school and Bapoojee went to the shop. Rekha learned to not speak of it all. Strangely, no one ever mentioned it, not Bapoojee, not Ba and even Babookaka never brought up the subject again. Her initial joy was replaced by a desperate hope. So she kept her dreams to herself in a place in her heart, in the same place where hope lived. There was nothing else to do but work and wait.

One afternoon, Rekha was on her hands and knees scrubbing the bathroom floor with hot water and a bristled brush. Ba was nearby in the kitchen preparing the supper.

"Now don't forget to clean in the corners, everyone's hair always get stuck in the corners and don't forget to clear the drains. I will check the bathroom after you are done. Oh, that baby is not well today. She's up again." Ba left the pots on the stove and rushed to the bedroom.

"Watch the food, Rekha," she called out.

"Jee, Ba," she answered into the floor as she finished scrubbing dirt off the ceramic tiles, her mother did not wait for her answer and was already in her room. Rekha got an old straightened wire hanger to pull out the hair stuck in the drain. She struggled to fish out the clumps of hair and whatever else people left in the sink. She pushed and pulled, finally she was successful and drew out the wire which had a large glop of hair attached. She knew why the drain had smelled so bad? She stopped and realised that it was not hair stinking but the unmistakable stench of burnt rice. The smell filled the kitchen and if she could smell it, then it was beyond fixing now. She rushed to the stove and dropped the wire on the kitchen floor. She grabbed the handle of the pot and realised too late she had forgotten to use a cloth. She shrieked with pain and let it go. The rice spilled onto the stove and floor. The smell of burned rice wafted from the stove again as the white kernels were smoked dark brown.

She took a second to think about cleaning the mess or should she be saving her hand from the searing pain. The pain made the decision for her; she rushed to the basin and put her hand under the cold water. With her good hand, she held her burnt hand steady under the water. The intensity of pain eased slightly, but not enough so that she couldn't stop the tears from flowing.

"What have you done?" Ba moved the remaining pots from the stove and used a wet kitchen cloth to sweep off the burning rice from the stove.

"I...I tried to save the rice...but I burned my hand..." she cried.

"I told you to watch the food!"

"I tried, Ba, but..."

"But nothing, you stupid girl!" Ba spied the wire on the floor and picked it up. She took a few steps toward Rekha, lifted her arm and swung. Rekha, standing with her hand under the water, instinctively turned her face away from her mother and crouched into a semi-foetal position standing. She held onto the tap afraid she would fly across the room otherwise. She smacked her head on the tap in the process, stunning her. She told herself that she should move, run, scream, do something, do anything to stop her mother. But she couldn't move, she was frozen. The wire landed again and again on her back and on her legs. Ba had lost control. She was swearing and calling her horrible names, in Gujarati and Afrikaans. Her mother was not thinking. But then, her mother never did think when she was angry, she just reacted.

Rekha couldn't remember much. She didn't remember how long she stood there or even when her mother had stopped beating her and had walked away. Her sight was blurry, from her tears still flowing and the blood which ran down her face from her forehead. Her hands were numb from holding onto the tap so tight and so long. As she released them, she felt the tingling of the blood flowing back into her joints. She straightened her body from the crouched position and winced with every movement. She realised that she was bleeding all over the sink and floor. She supposed it came from her gash on her forehead and attempted to clean it up with a rag in one hand and pressing the gash with her other hand. But the blood kept splattering on the floor every time she moved or turned. Then it dawned on her, she was bleeding from body, her arms, her legs and her back. Any place where that wire had landed. They were like tiny streams linked up and running to nowhere. She moved to the bathroom as quickly as possible to take off her dress and wash it before the bloodstains were became permanent. She saw herself in the mirror and cried out in horror and shame. All she could see was red. Red on her face from her forehead injury and red on her back and dress.

"Rekha? Oh God! What happened!?" Jyoti stood in the doorway of the bathroom with a look of horror and disbelief. She had just arrived from school.

"I...I burned the rice," Rekha replied simply. Her chin trembling and eyes full of fresh tears. Jyoti's eyes filled with tears and understanding. They did not speak. There was nothing to say. Her younger sibling eased the wet clinging dress from her back. The dress was shred and stained beyond repair. Rekha stood like a baby and let her body be wiped with a cold washcloth. She winced with every touch but tried to be silent. She moaned, biting her lip to stop herself from crying out when Jyoti dressed her in a fresh clean nightgown. She was gently placed in bed face down. Some salve was gently rubbed onto her burned hand and open gashes on her body. The window was shut, the curtains were drawn and the door was closed. It was dark in the room but Rekha did not notice or care. She had drifted off to another place far away, a place where she did not feel pain or fear. She had visions and heard voices. Blurred images of people coming to her, laughing and giggling about some joke they had shared. She had other visions, one that was very scary, of someone crying behind a closed door, but she couldn't reach the door. It was beyond her reach. The visions continued to a few days and nights, but were strongest in the night when the house silent and dark. She didn't know that the cries and wails she heard were coming from her. And Jyoti tried her hardest to calm and soothe her, with songs and humming, gently rubbing her hands or forehead, until the cries softened to a whimpering.

Chapter 6

The mood of the house was sombre and quiet for days. The one person oblivious to the atmosphere was the baby, cooing and crying, telling the house when she was hungry or wet. Jyoti stayed home from school, nursing and feeding Rekha, while doing all the chores that Rekha normally did. Her absence from the kitchen was explained to the boys and the other family members as "woman problems." No specific explanations, no doctor required. Just ill, not well enough to work or get up from bed. The same story was given to Babookaka who didn't question such *female* problems. Ba continued as normal, never admitting or denying her actions. Not making any attempts to amend the damage.

Rekha had cocooned into herself, no conversation, no acknowledgement of her father who came to see her every day, sometimes even twice a day. Some days, he brought chocolates and chatted about the customers who had come that day, sometimes he just sat next to her and ran his hand over her forehead softly. Rekha thought, at times, he was trying rub out the pain or even rub out the entire event from her mind. Silence seemed to be the healer, no words were spoken or necessary. Not by Rekha, not by Jyoti, not by Bapoojee and especially not by Ba. If Bapoojee had reprimanded his wife, no one knew or heard of it. Occasionally, late into the night, loud rumblings from the parents' bedroom filtered down the hallway. These were the nights when Bapoojee would come back from his social nights with his friends. The socials consisted of the older men sitting around, talking, drinking and playing cards until late. Nothing was heard from Rekha. The tears had stopped flowing, replaced by a calm silence. Only Jyoti could make her speak, if only in monosyllables, answering to questions of needing or wanting anything for the body. Otherwise the silence continued.

After a week, Rekha finally got out of bed and slowly made her way to the kitchen to eat and to the bathroom have to a shower. Then, by the second week, much to Jyoti's surprise, Rekha started to sit up in the bed and talk to her occasionally. Jyoti was usually the chattier one of the two and always had something to say. So, Jyoti always found something to say to Rekha, something about the boys, the shop or anything that had happened at school in the weeks before. After Jyoti finished the chores for the day, Jyoti would make a nice cup of *chaa* for the two of them and they would go outside with the baby, put her on a piece of cardboard covered with a blanket and have their tea in the sun. The sun felt good on her back, it felt like someone was bathing her in a healing light. They both thoroughly enjoyed this time of the day and it went on for a good week. Ba was not to be heard, quiet in her room or helping with the stock in the shop. The girls could feel her venom, and they were sure that she did not like it one bit. They knew because, normally, this act of indulgence would bring her wrath down on them, swiftly and cruelly. They had heard her complain many times before about sitting in the sun.

"What do you think? This is a boarding house or a hotel? You can't just sit outside and get dark? Who do you think will marry a *khari* – black girl? What kind of man would even look at you if you are so dark?" She would taunt them. "I don't want you sitting outside unless you are doing work," they were told continuously. But this time it didn't happen. At first, they were fearful that they would get caught and be punished. They only went outside if all the housework required it and never for any other reason. Without any reprimands coming their way, they cautiously made it a daily ritual for a week and were happy and relieved for this precious moment.

Jyoti and Bapoojee never knew or even imagined how Rekha made herself get up from bed and come out of the darkness and silence. They did not know that she replayed and relived the events that led had up the day before the beating. She remembered making all the tasty pastries and how much fun she and Jyoti had preparing them. She remembered cleaning the house and making the *chaa*, taking out the good dishes for the visitors. And then she replayed the final day of the visitors arriving, her nervousness of seeing the boy and finally the realisation of what it all meant. A promise of her life and her future with this boy. This and only this had kept Rekha from allowing her mother's abuse from breaking her. It was not easy. At first, there was only dark despair in her mind and in her heart. But slowly, every night and sometimes day, she remembered the promise and it slowly pushed out the morose gloom of her life and held the light of promise close to her heart. By the third week, Rekha was soon back to her full duty of chores and Jyoti went back to school. Jyoti didn't want to go. She was afraid for Rekha, afraid her mother would go too far again. She had taken good care of her sister. Rekha's back was almost completely healed. She still had scars, and some aches when she carried heavy loads, but they aches would stop and the scars which would hopefully fade. Jyoti made sure she used every homemade remedy she could think of and meticulously applied the medicine to her sister's back every night. Rekha was grateful but she could not find the words that could express her gratitude. Sometimes, words were not enough or just too inadequate.

"You have to go back to school Jyoti," Rekha said to Jyoti after breakfast one Sunday morning, two weeks after the incident. They stood side by side over the kitchen basin, one washing and the other drying the dishes.

"No, I won't leave you," Jyoti whispered.

"I am fine, it doesn't hurt so much now, I can do the work," Rekha argued back.

"I know, but..." Jyoti shut her eyes, in an attempt to stop the flash vision of the long scars on her sister's back, luckily the scars were fading day by day. Jyoti was relieved to know that no one would see them. And Rekha would not have to hide her back from anyone, especially her future husband, and have to explain how she got them.

"No buts, you must go. You must learn and get smarter. I know you want to work in the shop and help Bapoojee, you must do your studies first." Rekha turned and looked at her sister, face to face, "Look at me!" she ordered.

Until then, they had conversed without looking at each other, both trying to avoid the pain of the obvious truth. Jyoti stopped washing, turned to Rekha, looked down at her hands which were shaking a little and lifted her eyes. Her eyes pooled with water, nothing could stop them, nothing else to do but let them flow down her cheeks. Her face was damp with tears, she could not hide her fear.

"But...Ba," Jyoti choked on her words.

"She cannot do anything to me. I am stronger than she thinks. And one day soon, I will leave her house of Hell," Rekha answered vehemently.

She had not realised how strongly she felt about her mother and how determined she was until she had said these words out loud. Jyoti nodded in understanding and silently accepted her sister's declaration of independence. The next day, Rekha prepared the breakfast for the family. Jyoti prepared for school, pressed her blouse and pinafore, brushed her black shoes until they shined. She ate her breakfast of *chaa* and rusks, gave a small smile for Rekha before she left for school with her brothers to join the outside world. The girls had decided, without much discussion, they would support each other no matter what. They would strive for what they wanted in life. If marrying and having children was what Rekha wanted and needed, that was what she would get. If Jyoti wanted to work alongside her father in the family business, then that was what she would do. No one, especially their domineering and abusive mother, would get in their way. They went on with their life as before. One at school, doing her lessons and chores when she came home and the other doing her chores at home and enjoying the companionship of her sister. To Rekha, life was a series of Mondays which consisted of chores and more chores, with the occasional break of the Saturday and Sunday which usually brought visitors, breaking the monotony of life. But then again, the chores were always waiting for her after the fun. Secretly, she wished with all her heart that Bharat and his family would come to visit. She fantasised that they could not wait for her and demanded that she come with them that day. But they never did. There was never any discussion of that family or of the engagement.

That same week that Jyoti went back to school, Bapoojee began to stop in the kitchen around mid-morning asking for a cup of *chaa*. He would take his time, assuring Rekha that Babookaka had everything under control and the shop was not busy. He passed his time, while she did her chores in the kitchen. As always, the radio was switched on the Indian channel.

"Do you hear the love in his voice? Oh, but the words are so sad…he is pining for her and she will not acknowledge their destiny to be together forever…" He sighed to himself, listening to the Indian songs from the latest black and white Hindi film on the wireless radio. Other times he would listen the BBC news, to hear what was going on in the world, other times he just talked. This routine became their time together, father and daughter. Rekha looked forward to this time of day. He would tell her the stories of the customers, the Whites, some with refined manners who talked to everyone with respect and others who looked down at the Coloureds, Indians and Blacks, as if they were cockroaches. He would tell her how he would catch the poor Indian children stealing from him, shouting at them and throwing them out of the shop. He failed to mention that when they came back, he would give them a small sweet. Many times he would get Black children, house servants, in the shop. They would come on shopping errands for small items such as sugar or tinned jam, with strict instructions from their house mistress, Indian or White. Bapoojee could not resist and would quietly, without fuss, slip them a small sweet for their walk back to their masters.

"Have I ever told you the story of how I came to this Africa?" he asked Rekha one day.

"No Bapoojee, but please tell me," Rekha urged, she could not contain her excitement, as she quickly set his *chaa* and biscuits down on the table for his mid-morning snack.

And he began his story of how he came to South Africa. He had saved money for few years, working as a clerk in a sari shop in Surat, a major town half a day's travel from Bombay, India. His family owned a farm and grew vegetables, in a small village outside Surat. They grew just enough to pay for the house, the land and essentials. After his parents found him a suitable bride from a neighbouring village, he decided to leave India. He had heard news from the customers and others in town about places such as South Africa, a small British colony at the bottom of Africa. He heard stories about this beautiful country, and the great opportunities for anyone willing to work hard and had good mind for business. The British Empire was offering land in the 1920s, in Natal, to the lucky few if they stayed after ten years. Many Indians came to South Africa as indentured slaves to work in the sugar plantations. Bapoojee was lucky, he had money and a desire to make something of himself, as he put it. He was what the Whites called a "passenger Indian." He spoke of the long journey from Surat to Bombay by train and then a large sailing vessel from there to Zanzibar and then another ship to Mozambique and then another long train journey to Johannesburg. This is where Bapoojee started a business and a family and planted his roots.

A few times, Bapoojee spoke of a certain group of people who wanted to change South Africa. They wanted to help the Blacks and Indians give them rights, freedom and a better life. He never mentioned names or what the group was called. He talked of Mahatma Gandhi, a young lawyer who had come from India to practice law in South Africa. Gandhi spoke of non-violence protests against the white masters and how everyone has control over their own destiny.

Rekha knew that she was not to repeat whatever he told her. He always spoke with a hush and quickly, in case someone would overhear him. Rekha didn't understand most of what her father spoke of. Why did the Indians and Blacks need more freedom? Didn't they have jobs and homes? Didn't the Blacks get fed by their masters and get lodging? Who was this Gandhi person? It was all too much for her to worry about. She just wanted to know when she would be leaving and getting married. Maybe, this group could help her get her freedom and get control over her own destiny. But that was silly, why would they help women? Men were always in control. They were the educated ones; they earned the money and they made the rules. Most nights, as she lay her head down on her pillow and rested her exhausted body, Rekha would think of Bharat and wonder what he was doing. *Was he happy? Was he a clever student at school? Was he having a good life? Was he wondering about her? When would he come back to visit?*

Chapter 7

The days and months carried on as they always did for Rekha, cooking and cleaning. Her least favourite chore was washing the family laundry. Most mornings, right after cleaning up the breakfast mess, she collected all the dirty clothes and the dirty smelly cloth nappies. She tried very hard to not be sick when carrying those filthy nappies. Sometimes Ba would forget, or didn't have the time, to rinse the shit nappies at night and they made a horrible stink after sitting in the nappy pail overnight. She rolled out a large tin drum outside, carried two kettles of hot water, one by one, from the black stove, filling the tin drum with hot and cold water. She used a bar of carbolic soap and a brush and scrubbed the clothes until they were clean. Once the scrubbing was done, the clothes had to be rinsed and hung with wooden pegs, letting the midday sun dry the clothes. Apart from the back breaking work of lifting and bending, the soap burned her hands leaving them raw and pulsing. Rekha would coat her hands in Vaseline to ease the pain and redness. By late afternoon, her hands were better and the sun had done its job, drying and heating the clothes and giving them a distinct smell from the African breeze and sun. The clothes, nappies and linens were collected and ironed with a hot flat iron. Every single item was ironed, the boys' school socks, the *broekies* – the under-garments worn closest the body, Ba's cotton saris, Bapoojee's work shirts and even the ribbons worn by Jyoti and herself. By the time the boys and Jyoti came home from school, fresh clean clothes were sitting on their beds waiting to start the cycle once again. Rekha often wondered to herself… *What would happen if I didn't do the laundry? Everyone would be in shock, no clean socks and shirts for school and work! How would they cope? That would catch them!* But this fantasy was short-lived, especially when Ba's footsteps were heard in close range traveling from room to room.

As usual, Bapoojee came for his usual mid-morning *chaa*, sat down and helped himself to the sugar biscuits Rekha put on the table. He was quiet, very unusual for Bapoojee, taking one biscuit at time, dipping his biscuits in his *chaa* and swallowing them whole before they fell apart in his hand. He looked at Rekha, smiled and with a twinkle in his eye, went back to eating. He did this a couple of times.

"Bapoojee, what is it?" queried Rekha. She had butterflies in the stomach, she sensed something was up. *But what? Could it be? Bharat and his family were finally coming to visit! How could her father tease her so?*

"These are *lekker* my girl! I wonder how many I can eat today? I hope there more biscuit tins somewhere, we are going to need them…" he said soberly looking at his daughter.

Rekha searched his face for a clue, hesitantly looked up at the cupboards to confirm that there was a couple biscuit tins, and brought her gaze back to her father. His face now had a broad open mouth and smiling eyes. He sat back in his chair and hooked his thumbs into his vest and puffed out his chest...he looked like he was ready to burst with happiness.

"Bapoojee, please...you must tell me, who is coming!?" she pleaded. He looked at her quizzically and wondering what she was talking about and realised what she was thinking.

"No *dikri*, not visitors. We are going to have a wedding in the family! What a joyous occasion! My brother's daughter, your cousin, Manju is getting married! Your Babookaka and Bhartikaki have finally agreed and the date is set! Manjuben is marrying that boy from that small town, the family owns a fruit stall...you must remember him?" asked Bapoojee with a twinkle in his eye.

"Yes, I remember Kaka speaking of the match a while ago," she quietly confirmed.

He was truly pleased and rambled on about the endless details of the wedding. Rekha listened with a smile on her face, not showing her disappointment and pain. *No, no. She will not be seeing her Bharat again.* She hoped desperately that her disappointment did not show on her face. She got up from the table, keeping her hands busy with dirty dishes and checking the food on the stove. Nodding and smiling while her father chatted away.

"What is this? Who is getting married?" Ba questioned as she walked into the kitchen. Bapoojee filled her in with all the glorious details. An animated and long discussion began about the guest list, food, the *brahmin* that would be conducting the marriage ceremony. Rekha quietly left them to it and mumbled something about checking the laundry on the line. She knew before she touched the clothes that they were wet. She hid between the hanging clothes and covered her face with her hands to hide the tears that escaped. They came fast and hot on her face. *What was wrong with her?* She should be happy for Manjuben, her parents and her father. At least, no one can speak ill of the family. The honour of marriage for an Indian girl was above and beyond anything else. There was nothing else. Manjuben will be a happily married woman with a husband and children to care for carry who will bear his family name forever. What an accomplishment!

But why couldn't it be her? She already knew the answer to her own question. She was too young still and she had to wait. Wait for what was promised to her.

Stop! She chided herself, she had to stop being so selfish, her time will come. *Be patient!* Be happy for Manjuben and Babookaka and kaki. They were good people, they were her family, she must be happy for them. Her mind was made up and she maintained a happy disposition from that day onward, remembering that her day will soon come.

That Saturday, Rekha and her family went to officially visit her uncle's family for afternoon c*haa*. First, they were there to congratulate the whole family on the exciting event and also to help organise the multitude of details that were involved in any wedding. Manju was quiet and shy about the whole thing. She went about making *chaa*, occasionally smiling and nodding her head at questions and compliments directed to her. But the conversation was, as usual, dominated by the adults.

"First things first," Babookaka started, "we have given the *brahmin* the birth dates of both Manju and Rahul, her fiancé, he will give wedding dates by Monday."

"But we can begin to prepare, we can shop for the clothes, contact all the people we need to..." added Bapoojee. Manju finished placing the table with cups, saucers, biscuits, *chevra* and the *chaa* for the adults. She looked around the room to make sure she had done everything needed and finally rested her gaze at her cousins, Rekha and Jyoti and winked at them. With a flick of her head, she indicated to go to the bedroom. They all got up slowly and moved in the direction the girls' bedroom.

"Ba, we are just going to my room for a while," Manjuben informed Bhartikaki.

"*Ja dikri,* you sit and relax with your sisters," Bhartikaki said, her voice full of pride and love. Rekha had always marvelled at her auntie and how kind she was to her children, especially the girls. *What made her so different to her own mother?* Sometimes, Rekha secretly wished she was Bhartikaki's daughter...her life would be so different. But not in this lifetime, maybe in her next life, she would be luckier.

Rekha took the sleeping baby from her Ba's arms and went with Manjuben and all the girls settled themselves in various positions of sitting and reclining on the two beds in the room. They chatted about the wedding, the clothes and the jewellery that Manjuben would need and receive. They teased Manjuben about her fiancé and giggled away for a few hours. All the while, Rekha scrutinised her cousin's face...she acted the same and looked the same, but something was different, she just couldn't quite figure out what it was. Manjuben caught the questioning gaze of Rekha and smiled at her. Rekha quickly lowered her eyes, pretending to check the baby as she slept in her lap, embarrassed to have been caught staring at her cousin.

"Rekhaben," Manjuben smiled shyly and said, "soon it will be your turn and we will be two old married ladies."

Rekha's breath was taken away, quickly taking in Manjuben's smile, and ducked her face down now again. She turned away from all the eyes in the room and placed the baby on the bed. She was mortified, until this moment no one had spoken of her engagement. *How did Manjuben know? Now everyone would know.*

Rekha turned to touch the baby to see if the excitement in the room had awakened her from her nap. She kept her hand on the baby's back, half hiding from the questioning faces and half keeping an eye on the baby. The baby was, of course, oblivious to the noise and slept soundly between pillows. They all began chattering at once, peppering questions to Rekha.

"Is it true?"

"When did this happen?"

"Who is the boy?"

"This is too exciting, two weddings in one family!"

Jyoti felt her sister's embarrassment and reluctance to speak and she piped up.

"Yes, it is true and you all know the boy, the one from the Lala family."

"You mean Bharat!?" squealed one of the young girls, who joined them, from the house next door.

"Yes…that is the one," answered Jyoti.

Their squealing turned into giggling and swift exchange of smiles and eye rolling.

"What a dream."

"He is so smart and handsome…I see him all the time…playing with my brothers at school."

Rekha wanted to melt into the ground or hide in the wardrobe, go anywhere and not hear all this nonsense! Manjuben sensed her uneasiness and settled the girls down.

"Now, now, you mustn't go on like this, girls; it has just been decided and Rekha and Bharat won't be getting married for a while, he is still in school…so stop all this silly chatter!"

Rekha released a heavy sigh, not realising that she had been holding her breath for a while. She turned to Manjuben and sent a swift smile in her direction, showing her gratitude.

"Can we talk about what we are going to wear to your wedding Manjuben?" asked the one of the girls.

"Of course you can and I want to hear what everyone is going to wear…" replied Manjuben.

The conversation turned to fabrics and colours, and patterns of dresses, ribbons and socks and who was getting new shoes. Rekha and Jyoti joined the lively discussion, because sewing dresses and clothing was one of their favourite things to do and talk about.

The adults were soon done talking and working out all the details the lists upon lists of things to get done for the upcoming nuptials. It was time to go home. Rekha picked up the baby, who was slowly waking from her nap and handed her to her father.

"Come *dikri,* come, did you have a good nap?" her father cooed at the baby. The baby rubbed her eyes and gave her father a tired smile. Bapoojee beamed back at her.

Rekha and Jyoti quickly helped Manjuben clear things up in the kitchen and left her to wash up the dishes.

"Now, you take care, Rekha," Manjuben smiled at her as if the two of them belonged to a special club. As usual, Rekha was mute and didn't know what to say, especially in front of the adults and her sister. Her mother looked at Rekha with a curious grin, as if she was part of the conversation. As soon as Babookaka closed the door, Ba pulled Rekha from everyone's earshot.

"What was that nonsense about!?" Ba asked, "Is she filling your head with silly stories?"

"No, no, Ba. She was just being nice. You know what she is like." Rekha defended Manjuben's actions. Ba seemed satisfied with her answer and walked ahead to walk with the boys and Bapoojee. Jyoti had noticed her sister and mother in conversation and had purposely slowed her steps to make sure Rekha was alright.

"Anything wrong?" she inquired.

"Nothing…nothing at all. She was just asking about Manjuben," she assured her sister with a tight smile, watching her mother walk away. The family walked home together, all chattering away about the many tasks ahead of them. All of them, except Rekha who was silent, lost in her own thoughts. Words kept swirling around her head, not being able to concentrate on one, they moved so quickly…wedding, handsome boy, wife, saris and jewellery and love, there was that word. Love. It was too much to take in, what did she know of Love? That was for the film stars and the singers on the radio and for white people. She shook her head and scolded herself to stop thinking about such nonsense! She will do what is expected of her and keep her husband happy. When they reached home, Rekha waited her turn to wash her feet, face and dressed into her nightie, slipped into bed with her sister and fell sound asleep. Her life was suddenly too complicated and she wasn't even married yet. Her thoughts made her mind and body heavy and tired. *Why was she so tired all of the sudden?* Rekha hoped that she would be as happy as Manjuben when it was her turn. *Would she be happy? Would her husband treat her like they sang about in the love songs she heard on the radio? Of course!* She chided herself, married life has to be better than how she was living now. Nobody could be as bad as her mother.

Chapter 8

The days and nights were spent fulfilling the many demands their mother placed on them. Every spare moment, outside of the household chores and wedding tasks were spent on cutting and sewing the two dresses the sisters were going to wear for the wedding. They had asked their father for some patterns that were sold in their shop. From the newest patterns, they chose a calf-length dress with a wide skirt. Rekha and Jyoti would be wearing soft cream-coloured dresses. Rekha's dress would have a thick sky-blue ribbon that hugged her waist and a sweetheart neckline and short puffy sleeves. She would be wearing matching sky-blue ribbons on her braids. The dress was made out of soft cream chiffon for the outside layer, with a stiff petticoat under of the same colour with some crinoline underneath to puff up the skirt. Jyoti's dress was a little plainer with less crinoline, a yellow ribbon and a square neckline. As the older sister and as an engaged young girl, it was understood that Rekha had to shine for everyone, especially Bharat and his family. Even their mother did not balk at the cost of the material and the amount of time they gave to the details of sewing. Most evenings, after all the chores were done, the two girls went straight to their room, chatting and sewing quietly by the one bulb that hung from their bedroom ceiling. They sewed late into the night and stopping only when their eyes hurt from the strain and the stitches were blurring. But the excitement of the wedding kept them energetic and happy every morning and day, until that special day arrived.

The two families spent a lot of time together to synchronise their efforts to make everything exactly right for Manjuben and her wedding. The family had to be and look united, while working like dogs, day and night to complete all the necessary jobs. Manjuben and the two girls spent more time together and became closer than they ever imagined. Rekha loved going to Manjuben's house and being part of her family. No one there was being scolded, verbally abused and beaten. Everyone seemed so happy to see each other and talk to each other about their school days, work and just local news and gossip that floated from one household to the next. Nothing was a secret in their community. Faces were always peering from windows and ears were always perked ready to hear what was happening in so and so's house and who did what to who. Rekha couldn't remember that last time she was so happy. She was riding the "high" of Manjuben's wedding and she didn't want to come down. She thought, *this was what it felt like to married, everyone was just so happy all the time!* Rekha imagined her wedding preparations would be just as hectic but equally exciting for all, especially her, being the bride-to-be.

One day, Jyoti had to stay home to look after the baby, who was feeling at odds, with a fever, crying bouts and diarrhoea. Ba concluded with maternal confidence that the baby was probably teething. But only Jyoti could console the baby and she remained at home to help. Rekha and her father went to, which was now called the "wedding house", to finalise details. Manjuben and her family greeted them both smiles and hugs. There was a lot of masculine back-slapping between the two brothers, congratulating themselves on a job well done. The women and girls knew who really did all the work but let them puff up like peacocks, they didn't have the heart to smother the love and cheer going around.

While the boasting continued with a drink of scotch for the men. Manjuben took Rekha quietly by the hand to her room.

"I want to show you something." Manjuben went to the corner of her room and lifted some blankets and sheets from a metal box.

"What is it?" Rekha asked with a whisper and big round eyes, she was curious beyond curious.

"My trousseau…you will also have one of these."

"A trou…what?"

"You know, a trousseau…It is *White* term used to describe all the clothes I will need when I go to my in-laws house," she turned to gently lift numerous garments, sari after sari, blouses, the match bangles and also nightgowns, skirts and dresses and shoes, she placed them on her bed for Rekha to see.

"Really? Who gave that to you? Your fiancée?" Rekha asked in rapid succession, she couldn't believe the gorgeous colours and fabrics that were floating in front of her eyes.

"No, no silly girl. My parents took me shopping and we bought all these things together. My father wants me to make a good impression on the in-laws."

"But isn't it very expensive? How can they afford all these things!?" Rekha asked while gawking at the collection of clothes on the bed.

"Well, yes, but we have been saving for a long time and buying slowly," Manjuben explained with a confident smile, "I am sure your father and mother are also saving money for your wedding and trousseau right now."

"But how can they? We have been so busy with your wedding preparations and buying things for ourselves, new shoes for the boys, material for our dresses, and all that food to feed the wedding guests…and Bapoojee and Ba have said nothing to me!" Rekha exclaimed.

"Don't worry, I am sure they are getting ready, your father helped my father keep money aside for my wedding for a long time, even when they didn't know who the boy would be, but they knew that this day would come. Your father is so clever with numbers and money, you know," said Manjuben.

Rekha's gaze swept from to the trousseau and back to Manjuben and just smiled, brimming with pride for her father and knowing that she would be getting a trousseau just like Manjuben. In fact, Rekha beamed for the rest of the night, from the walk home, through the cranky reception she received from her sister and mother, who had spent the last few hours with the miserable baby. But Rekha was too happy to notice Jyoti's foul mood. She went straight to the bathroom to wash her face and changed for bed. She looked herself in the bathroom mirror and saw a very content happy girl there. In fact, Rekha was still beaming with a smile as her head touched the pillow, while dreams of beautiful clothes and a beautiful wedding floated in her head.

The following weeks pass quickly. The numerous ceremonies that led up to the final wedding day were full complicated events, with food, seating, outfits and lots of work. There was the *Piti*, the *Sangeet* and the *Ganesh puja* before the wedding day taking place on Sunday. Of course, the wedding had been planned to land on a Sunday when all the shops were closed and Rekha's father and Babookaka had the whole day and night to be at the wedding and take care of the details. The boy's side was probably doing the same things, completely immersed in their family and rituals. Most of Rekha's family and especially Manju's family didn't get much sleep. The visitors kept coming and going, staying for hours on end to help and celebrate the family's good fortune. Bapoojee split his time between the shop and helping his brother make sure that everything went exactly right without any hiccups He was also the man with the money, he took care of the bills and the people who were hired to do work. He had to take care of the *Brahmin*, making sure he was available, well fed and looked after before, during and after the ceremonies. He was essential for all the ceremonies, except the *Sangeet Garba* – a night of singing and folk dancing. Bapoojee had hired the band who would playing the music for the *Garba.* That consisted of a harmonium, small hand-held piano player, a couple of singers and a table, small drums, player. Although the Gujarati community was small in Johannesburg, there were still numerous families coming in from other towns and cities to attend the wedding. They came in at all hours of the day and night. Most expected food and drink, and at least a place to sleep for the first night. Some spent the first night with them and then would make arrangements with their family or friends. Rekha thought the flow of people would never end. And why were they staying with them? They were not even related...some Rekha had never seen before, but her parents knew all of them. Either from their family connections from India, or made friends with them when Rekha's parents arrived in South Africa. Rekha wanted to spend time with Manjuben, not at home cooking, cleaning and serving these visitors. *But, wanting, had nothing to do life. You did what you were told, without a question.* And that was exactly Rekha did. She worked and worked and prayed for when she and Jyoti would a few spare moments and they would beg to go see Manjuben. Her house was just as busy as theirs, with visitors and preparations taking place, all the closely related women of the family and the neighbours were at Manjuben's house every day to help with whatever needed to be done. Rekha envied her older cousin more and more as the special day approached. At times, wishing so hard that it was her getting married instead. *My day will come soon too!* Rekha had always considered Manjuben to be a pretty girl, not beautiful, but pretty. She had those lovely almond shaped eyes, with a small nose and a heart-shaped chin. She was taller than the average Indian girl, taller than her mother and brothers with just enough curves without looking too bony. But now, she was changing...Rekha couldn't stop looking at her. Manjuben was becoming more and more beautiful, by the day. She was radiant, a light was shining inside her and was oozing through her skin. Her eyes were shining, her skin glowed and a smile never left her face. Jyoti and Rekha spoke about this during their evening chats, while in bed. *How could be possible?* Jyoti noticed it as well.

"Do you think she is using a special cream?" asked Jyoti, "you know, one of those expensive ones the white ladies use?"

"I really don't know, where would she get it from?" Rekha answered, shaking her head.

"Maybe Kaka and Kaki went to Johannesburg town and bought it there?"

"No, they would not be allowed in the shops! They are for Whites only!" explained Rekha.

"Maybe they asked one of the white salesmen to come to our shop to buy it…" ventured Jyoti, very pleased with herself for coming up with such a convoluted scheme.

Their questions continued, back and forth, until they both were too tired, and eventually one of them slept without replying to the other and the other giving up as well.

Chapter 9

The night of the *Sangeet Garba* had finally arrived, it was the biggest night…since anyone who was important, would be there to join in the festivities. Thankfully, everyone had forgotten or were too busy to ask Rekha about her engagement. She was very relieved, not knowing herself, what to think and what to say to people. Even Ba was in an exceptional mood and did not shout as much. Everyone was in a good mood with giggles and smiles and a lot of good-natured teasing. The boys dressed in their cleanest and recently pressed trousers, shirts and polished black shoes. The girls wearing their 'good' but old dresses with bleached white socks and pretty ribbons in their well-oiled and plaited hair. The family had to squeeze in the car with the smaller ones sitting on the laps of the bigger children. Ba sat in the front with baby on her lap. One of the boys would squeeze himself in the very rear in the small caboose. Rekha was quiet today, hiding her intense excitement. No one else knew what she knew, Bharat would be there, she was certain of this and that certainty caused her heart to beat faster than she thought possible.

Although the car journey was short, everyone piled out of car with a sigh of relief. They knew better not to complain, because, while other families had to walk or take a bus or depend on others for a lift to the event. They were the fortunate family and they did not need to be told or reminded. They quickly found Manjuben's family and the two families arranged themselves in the front row of the seating. The hall was small, which accommodated only a hundred people, a large crowd considering the small community of Gujaratis in and around Johannesburg. The hall was actually an old warehouse that was unused for a long time. It was on the border of the Indian and Whites area. The Whites would not stand for a crowd of Indians congregating in their neighbourhood with their oil and spice smells and loud ways. Bapoojee was very fortunate to have found out about it from one of his White suppliers. They had worked together for years and developed a trusting relationship. This kind of trust and relationship was very rare for any White person. Some would say that they were almost friends, but no one would dare say anything like that out loud. That was unacceptable in this country. Bapoojee was lucky to get this place for the price and he paid the full payment on his own. The rest of the community had donated whatever they could in terms of labour in fixing it up with fresh paint on the concrete walls and washing of the windows. Others over the past few years donated chairs and supplies that were needed to hold functions such as these. It had become the place where all the Indian functions were held. People would request and reserve the hall and Bapoojee would seldom take money for it. All he asked of these people was to donate money, whatever they could afford, which was collected and kept safe and recorded by Bapoojee and Babookaka. This money was then used to assist the poorer families who couldn't afford much for weddings and funerals and any function that was needed for the community at large. Rekha and her siblings had no idea about all of this until they were much older as adults and the next generation who kept the Gujarati community together.

The girls sat together and tried their best not to speak or act out of turn, in fear of incurring the wrath of their mother. She, of course, would not say anything in front of these people, but definitely show her disapproval in the next and following days to come. That unpredictable 'discipline' was what the girls feared the most. But they still enjoyed every moment, watching, appraising and analysing the outfits, the crowd, the hall and the music. It was splendidly full of colour, music and chatter. Rekha scanned the small crowds around the hall, while switching her gaze to the entrance, hoping she would get a glimpse of her betrothed.

"Do you see him?" Manjuben asked quietly enough that only Rekha could hear her.

"What! Who?" Rekha whispered out of the corner of her mouth, not turning her head to her cousin, but knowing who Manjuben referred to. She was shocked that anyone took notice that she was looking for him.

"No, no…he is not here," she whispered, face down, hands tightly wrapped together.

"Don't worry, I am sure he will show up," Manjuben assured.

Before Rekha think of what to say, Manjuben was distracted with the other girls' chatter.

They quietly giggled, hiding their smiles and laughter behind their hands, always conscious of the adults nearby. God Forbid, their parents heard what they were giggling about. Every now and again, Rekha heard words flitting and floating around...cute, handsome, tall, big nose...the listing of male attributes went on and on, mostly resulting in more nervous laughter.

The older women and newly married girls got up to join in the folk-dancing. The men on the dance floor were older single men and middle-aged married men. Rekha watched intently as they whirled round and round. The *tabla* player increased the speed of the beat and the colours of the saris and the suits of the men began in blur in one long spectacular stream of rainbow colours. The voices of the singers rose with each round the dancers made. It was difficult to focus on one face or person. Rekha's struggled to her see and looked to the back of the room near the exit...her heart skipped a beat. It was him – Bharat. Earlier, she had denied herself the hope of seeing him tonight, but there he was. *Did he see her? Is he looking for her?* He stood with his friends, leaning on the wall, looking awkward, wanting to melt away. Some of the older boys were doing exactly what the girls were doing –pointing, laughing, and admiring the crowd, especially the girls. He was wearing a white shirt, black trousers (a little short and tight for him), white socks and polished well-worn shoes. All standard attire for a boy his age for weddings, funerals and prayers.

Quickly, Rekha checked to see what Ba was doing. She was deep in conversation with an older woman related to them in some way, both most definitely gossiping about another family member. Rekha's gaze flitted back to Bharat...he was really here and he looked so handsome. She couldn't stop looking at him. She studied him to memorise every angle of his face and his hair, his hands and his facial expressions. The last encounter they had, at their engagement, she only remembered his hands and feet, not daring to look up.

"Rekha, can you please come to the toilets with me?" But Rekha didn't hear Manjuben, she was so engrossed in her voyeurism.

"Rekha!" Jyoti pinched her arm, "Go with Manjuben to the toilets, you know she can't go alone…" whined her sister, not wanting to be chosen in case she missed any of the festivities.

Rekha looked at Manjuben and her sister in a slight daze. Not completely registering what they were saying.

"Ah…yes, of course," she replied.

"Good, I need help with my zipper," replied Manjuben got up and started walking toward the rear of the building, in the same direction where the boys were standing.

Rekha, quickly jumped up to catch up with Manjuben.

"Please wait for me, Manjuben." Rekha hissed as she scurried to catch up with her. Manjuben smiled to herself, as she slowed down just before they reached the boys and the exit door toward the toilet facilities behind the hall.

Numerous thoughts raced in Rekha's head…*Oh my…what should she do? Should she say hello? Should she smile at him? Will he remember her? What if someone sees her smiling at him? What if he talks to her? Think! What should she do…?*

"Hello Sanju, Bharat…you boys having a nice time?" Manjuben asked, coming to a full stop in front of the boys leaning against the wall. Rekha collected herself at the last second before she walked into Manjuben, being front and centre of a comical act. Mortified with fear and embarrassment, Rekha looked around and behind her, making sure nobody, namely her mother, was watching her.

The boys were shocked that anyone, especially a girl/woman, let alone the girl who was getting married would even talk to them. Funnily, they thought themselves invisible…

"Ah…ya, I mean, yes…it is nice," Sanju answered awkwardly. He gave Bharat a look, hoping that he will say something to help him. But Bharat was mute and determinedly examined his scuffed shoes.

"They look nice, don't they look *smart* Rekha?" Manjuben commented, while looking back at Rekha with a grin. Rekha felt her stomach rising and reaching her throat, desperately trying not to vomit at their feet. With an audible gulp, she swallowed the bile climbing up her throat and managed to pull the muscles of her mouth into a semi-grin, looking ridiculous as she felt and peeked out from behind Manjuben. Bharat looked up hearing her name and they both had an instant of connecting gaze. Bharat quickly went back to examining his scuffed shoes.

"Hey man, isn't she the one? That girl you told me about?" Sanju nudged Bharat with his elbow. Both Manjuben and Rekha looked at each other in surprise and back at the boys. Rekha's heart leaped with excitement and pride…*He talked about me…he knows who I am.*

"No! no…" Bharat mumbled looking everywhere but at Rekha.

"Not her! She is too fat," he added emphatically and looked directly at Rekha, daring her to say anything.

Rekha felt the knife of rejection slice through her heart, her ears burning with heat in embarrassment. She ran past them all to the exit, hoping she could make it to the toilets before the flood of tears betrayed her pain.

"That was mean…how could you?" Manjuben hissed at Bharat as she raced after Rekha.

Manjuben arrived in the ladies and thought for a second it was empty. Rekha was nowhere to be seen. As she turned to leave, she heard the soft cries coming from the last stall. Rekha sat on the toilet seat, with her hands covering her face, trying to muffle her sobs and cover her face from the shame and humiliation.

"Don't cry, he is just a stupid boy. He doesn't didn't mean it. Please, please don't cry," Manjuben whispered to Rekha, soothing her with a gentle rub on her back and head.

Rekha swallowed the saliva building up in her mouth and grimaced, trying to swallow the huge lump sitting at the top of her throat. She opened her hands wet with tears, desperately trying to contain the hurt and pain. She had to control herself. The last thing she needed was her mother hearing about this and giving her a good hiding for looking at the boys!? Not to mention causing a scene in a public place.

"Why? But why did he do it?" she asked Manjuben, her face still hidden in her hands.

"Boys are silly, and then they turn into stupid men…I know you don't believe me but it is true, one day you will understand," Manjuben answered with a reassuring smile.

Rekha looked at her with disbelief. *Manjuben thinks men are stupid!? Does she know what she is saying? Ba would be so angry if she heard this nonsense!*

"What are you saying Manjuben? He is my betrothed... my future husband!" Rekha replied with indignation, her face instantly changed from hurt to defiance and pride.

Manjuben took a moment before replying, deciding how to explain the complexities of men and women and relationships, but saw how naïve Rekha still was and smiled.

"You are right Rekha...maybe he made a mistake, maybe he is not feeling well, ya...that is probably what happened? Let us forget this and go out to watch the dancing." Manju grabbed Rekha's hand and led her back to the dancing and music.

The boys were not there when they came back into the hall. The music was louder and the beat was faster and the dancing area was filled, leaving little room to walk around. They squeezed through the crowd and reached their seats. The temperature of the hall had risen leaving everyone with slight sheen of sweat and many of the older aunties fanning themselves with whatever they could find. Jyoti looked at Rekha, whose eyes were red and swollen, with some concern and then at Manjuben.

"What is wrong? Why are your eyes red?" she whispered while she scrutinised her sister's face. Rekha did not know what to say, how to answer...her mind was a blank.

"Oh...she just stubbed her toe on the steps to the toilet. We put cold water on it, it is fine now," Manjuben quickly explained. "She is fine. Aren't you, Rekha?" forcing the lie.

Rekha nodded with some numbness in her heart and looked at her lap, not wanting to answer.

"Alright, but when we get home, we will put some *Zambuck* on it and check it again in the morning Rekha," Jyoti insisted, you don't want to have a swollen toe the next day.

"It is fine, really…" Rekha mumbled, still looking at her lap.

"Oh look!" Manjuben pointed to the band, trying to catch Jyoti's attention.

The moment ended, Jyoti got distracted by the new song and the swirling dancers. As Manjuben and Jyoti continued watching the dancing again, Rekha gained her composure and felt calmer. She spent the remaining hours of the evening watching the dancing and sporadically searching for him. But he was gone, he was not in the hall, she concluded. Her heart and head heavy with confusion about his behaviour, but convinced of her devotion to him, it all made her physically and emotionally tired. A few minutes shy of midnight, Bapoojee rounded up his children and they all piled in the car again, all drowsy and cranky from the long night. The baby sleeping in Ba's arms, she had fallen asleep hours ago, despite the noise, people and heat. Her mother took the front seat with the baby and the rest of the children crammed into the back. They boys were sleeping in the car with their heads lopping back and forth, as the car moved through the traffic toward home. Jyoti was the only one wide awake and she chattered all the way home about the evening.

"Did you see the sari that Dimple was wearing, it was so beautiful with gold sequins…" She squealed into her sister's ear. Rekha nodded and smiled indulgently to her chatter, but did not say much. She was lost in her own thoughts of the boy, one day to become a man, that she was going to marry. *Why did he behave like that? Maybe Manjuben was right, maybe he was not well or upset about something else. She had not done anything to him…it must be something else.* They reached home, quietly got out of the car, walked into the house and without too much nonsense, which was typical for the boys, prepared for bed. Rekha dressed for bed, undid her plaits and combed out her hair. She hung her dress and put her shoes away, washed her face and any remnants of the tears she had shed tonight. She stood at her wardrobe mirror, combing out her plaits with a comb and stared at herself and suddenly wondered…if *she too ugly for him? Was it her nose or her round face? Maybe, he didn't like her at all. But what could she do?* They were betrothed and nothing was going to change that. Rekha shook her head at the face in the mirror. *Stop it!* She scolded herself…*what can you do? You are just a girl without any control in this world.* All she could do was wait and see what tomorrow would bring. She turned away from the mirror and made her way to bed. Jyoti was already fast asleep, softly snoring, exhausted from the evening. As she put her head on the pillow and closed her eyes, she had one last thought and hope. *I will see him soon, at the wedding, and promised herself that it will be different. He would be different.*

Chapter 10

Rekha woke with a jolt, she heard something unfamiliar and strange and it was not the rooster or the birds. *Were the cats fighting again outside? Oh, the wedding! We have to get ready for the wedding*, Rekha jolted from her bed and walked to her wedding clothes which were ready, already hanging on the outside of her wardrobe. She looked longingly at her beautiful dress and the pretty ribbons she was to wear on her braids. She and her sister must have overslept! As she reached for her dress, she heard sounds coming from the kitchen, Ba must be grumbling about them sleeping in and not getting the breakfast ready. *Why hadn't she woken them up earlier?* There will be hell to pay and soon. She went to her bedroom door, slowly opening it, hoping that Ba was too busy with the baby's bottle to notice them not ready. But she heard something unfamiliar. Not the usual clatter of dishes and pots and water running. She heard wailing and moaning and hushed voices...*what or who was that?* Rekha looked back at the bed as Jyoti awoke and joined her at the door. They looked at each with ears to the door and hallway, both unsure but feeling some fear and trepidation.

"What is it? Who is that? Is Ba shouting about us? Are we late?" Jyoti questioned her sister, echoing the thoughts in her mind. Rekha shrugged her shoulders and shook her head in answer. They slowly approached the kitchen and saw Bapoojee turning from the front door to approach Ba who was sitting at the table. The front door was just shutting but they couldn't see who it was. Ba was rocking back and forth in the chair, her hand on her mouth, unsuccessfully trying to hold in the sounds that were coming from her. She was crying. Bapoojee stood with his hand reaching out, as if to touch her, soothe her. But he stopped when he saw he girls. He turned with his head down and leaned on the counter for support as if he was about to faint or fall.

"Bapoojee? What is it?" Rekha asked as she went to him. Jyoti went to their mother, not knowing what to do or say. Her father did not answer. He just stood at the counter, shaking his head. He could not speak. He turned his head to look at Rekha, his mouth moved but nothing was coming out. He turned his face away from her.

"Please, what is it? Tell us!" Rekha was feeling frantic and a little sick to her stomach. *What could it be? Is someone ill, did someone have an accident? Where was the baby?*

"Is it the baby?" she asked. Her father looked at her and who gave a short shake of the head.

"Who is it then? Who is sick?" she tugged at her father's shirt sleeve. She realised he was not completely dressed; he had just put on a shirt and trouser in a hurry. Ba was in her petticoat and blouse and but no sari. She had her housecoat on. She usually wore that late at night or in the early morning, when she was cleaning or cooking.

"I saw the door just shut, who came to the house?" Jyoti asked her parents, trying desperately to put the pieces of the puzzle together.

"Is Kaka sick? Or Kaki? Is it something to do with the wedding?"

"No...not them." Bapoojee finally broke his silence with a choked whisper, tears streaming down his face. "It's your cousin...Manju."

"What happened, is she sick? Did she hurt herself? We should go see her now!" Rekha felt her stomach clenching with pain. *What could have possibly happened?*

"No, no we can't," he replied.

"We can. I will dress the baby while you and Ba get ready. Jyoti can fix up some *chaa* for all of us. It won't take that long."

"You silly girl, we can't see her, she is dead!" shouted her mother, eyes flashing and red, as she rocked herself.

Jyoti recoiled from her and stood back in shock. Rekha looked at her mother in horror, shaking her head in denial.

"Why did you say that? That is not true. She is getting married today. Don't you want anyone to be happy!?" She spat out at her mother, not even considering the backlash from that outburst toward her mother.

"Bapoojee? Ba is lying, isn't she?" Rekha frantically gripping his arm, trying to get him to look at her. The boys now stood at the doorway from the hall, woken from the loud voices in the kitchen. They didn't speak. They had just caught the end of their mother's statement. They stood silent, no reaction, no tears. Boys were not to show emotion, they had all learned at a very young age – men were hard like rocks.

"My girl...your mother is not lying," he answered, "Manju is dead, she passed away this morning."

Rekha's head swirled and felt her body get light. She held tight onto her father's arm for support, hoping in vain that he was wrong. Jyoti wrapped her arms around her stomach, bent over, backing up against the wall. Their mother continued to moan and rock.

"What happened Bapoojee?"

"I don't want to scare you."

"You must tell us," asked Rekha, shutting her eyes, in an attempt to soften the blow of hearing how her beautiful Manjuben passed away.

"Well, it was an accident. Your uncle just came and told us. She was preparing the morning *chaa* and toast, she insisted on doing it one last time for her parents. Her hair caught on fire from the black stove. There was oil in a small pot on the stove and it splattered to her face and hair. She couldn't stop it...it, it spread too fast, they heard her screams too late..." He stopped, unable to speak and hung his head in grief.

"Stop, please don't tell anymore!" cried Jyoti from across the kitchen. "I can't hear anymore!" She bolted through the boys who gave way, from the kitchen and went down the hall to her parents' bedroom and shut the door. Trying to be as far away from the conversation as possible.

With tears streaming down her face, Rekha gripped her father's arm and pleaded.

"Please, can we go see her?"

"No, no one can see her. I must go now. I have to help your uncle make arrangements."

"What nonsense is this?" Ba hissed at Rekha, "You cannot go to the morgue! That is no place for women. You and your sister get the baby ready and we must go sit with Bhartikaki. She needs us now." Her mother just like that, stopped her moaning, wiped her face and got up from her chair. "There is so much to do…hurry now, get ready to go!"

"Jee Ba, I will get Jyoti and we will be ready just now." Rekha moved quickly. Her father tucked in his shirt into his trousers, pulled up his suspenders, grabbed his suit jacket and was out the door.

There was no time to waste, Manjuben's mother needed them. Both girls quickly washed their faces, dressed. One warmed the milk for the baby bottle, while the other changed the baby's nappie and dressed her. The boys were told to quickly get up without too much complaining or about the lack of breakfast and they got dressed. They all grabbed some biscuits and rusks to fill the stomachs as quickly as possible. Within ten minutes, the family was ready and was walking quietly with solemn faces toward Manju's house. Jyoti held onto the baby tightly, as if she were to fall out of her arms. This 'death thing' was new to them all. They had never had anyone close to their family pass away. It was always, someone old and far away in another town or in India, but never this close. Rekha was still having a difficult time believing what her parents told her. Secretly, she wished that Manju was alive and still couldn't comprehend how this could have happened. *What should she say to Kaki?* She was afraid. Afraid what was going to happen next, not knowing what was going to happen to the family or to her. They were a few doors away and they could hear the murmurs of the people standing outside, the crying and wailing of the women, they heard all this before they even reached the door. People were going in slowly, the men and boys of the community stood outside the house, not everyone could fit in the house. People made way for Ba, they recognised her and there was question to her presence and status as the older sister-in-law. She went in first, turned and looked at both the girls, as if to say…"*It will be okay*" or maybe trying to give the girls the courage to withstand what they were about to witness. Jyoti held the baby's head to make sure the eyes of the baby were fixed over her shoulder. As they stepped through the door and into the kitchen, they were assaulted with the smell of charred skin and hair and smoke. She desperately wanted to cover her mouth and nose, she tried to refrain from thinking that was the beautiful skin of Manjuben and her hair. As she followed her mother toward the bedroom where Manjuben's mother was lying down on the insistence of some ladies from the house next door. Rekha glanced to the stove and floor where the accident happened. Although, someone had tried to clean it up, there were traces of black hair and pieces of burned clothing here and there. And there was a smell, a horrible smell of cooked flesh and burnt hair. *Don't look! Stop looking!* She told herself, as she covered her nose and mouth. She felt her stomach revolting at the little breakfast she had this morning. She forced it back, instinctively knowing that this would not be the worst of this morning, the day or the days to come. She quickly turned to Jyoti, placing her hand on the baby's back who was beginning to whine, sensing that things were not right in this place. Jyoti was probably holding her too tight.

"Don't look down, keeping walking," she said as if they were walking a tightrope and they couldn't risk getting dizzy and falling.

When they reached the bedroom, they saw Ba holding Bhartikaki by the shoulders, their mother rubbing her back trying to soothe her pain. Kaki's eyes were red and swollen from hours of crying, her mouth was open, but no sound came out, as if she had lost her voice. Then a slow guttural noise came out, low and grating. It sounded something like when Ba had given birth to the baby and she was in so much pain, because the baby would not come out. The labour had been long and draining.

Rekha and Jyoti stood frozen at the door, not knowing what do. With eyes brimming with tears, she looked at Jyoti who was shaking her head and taking backward steps out of the room, with tears streaming down her face.

"No, I can't do this…I…can't," she cried out. With the baby in her arms, she left the room. At first, Rekha was surprised and irritated at the behaviour of her sister, but concluded it was better Jyoti had she left with the baby. The last thing they needed was an inconsolable screaming baby. The ladies in the other room will help look after them.

She turned back her mother and aunt and started walking toward them. The room was full of women, 2–3 sitting on the bed, a few others sitting on the floor, all of the crying and wailing at different times and intensity. They all knew Manjuben and the family, all good neighbours and ladies of the community. Rekha knew they were there, but everything was a blur and moving in slow motion. Step by step, she got closer to her aunt and mother. Rekha, her face wet with tears, reached out to touch her aunt's shoulder.

"Kaki?" she whispered, her throat choking with grief, "Kaki—" She could not finish the sentence. In fact, she did not even know what she was trying to say, it was all she could say. Manjuben's mother looked up at the sound of her voice and wiped her eyes and saw Rekha as if she had seen her in a long time. *It was just last night, wasn't it? They were all dancing and smiling...it felt so long ago.* Manjuben's mother looked up in a fog, not knowing who was talking to her. Once she realised who it was, she was alert and spoke.

"Rekha, *dikri*, bring my Manju to me," she pleaded to Rekha, she pulled at Rekha's hands.

"Bring her to me now, you know where she is, you must. My beautiful girl, where is she?" she questioned Rekha, with tears flowing like a river down her face and on her clothes and Ba's arm. Rekha's mother held her sister-in-law tight, soothing her as best she could. Rekha looked at her mother in confusion and fear, not knowing how to answer. Ba looked straight at Rekha and shook her head, to say, "Don't even think of lying to her." Rekha looked down at her aunt's hands tightly gripping hers.

"I...er...she is not here Kaki remember?" Rekha wanted to vomit right there from feeling so bad and thinking she will have to break this woman's heart. *Why was Ba so mean? Couldn't we just let her believe that Manjuben was not dead for a few minutes? Couldn't we all just pretend that she was not dead!?* She pleaded in her head. But she knew her mother, there would not be any softness about this. Her mother would not let this go if Rekha said or did the wrong thing here. Later, Rekha learned that Ba was not always so mean, but just knew and understood the reality of life and sometimes that included death. Unpleasant and ugly as it was. Rekha knew there was no easy way out for her here. Ba glared at her and willed her to give Kaki the truth.

"Kaki, I'm sorry but…Manjuben is gone…she is dead." Rekha choked on her words and ended her statement in a whisper, not quite believing what she was saying herself.

"Noooo! You lie!" wailed Kaki at Rekha and looked for support from Ba and the other women. Ba shook her head at her sister-in-law and softly spoke to her.

"*Bhabi*, she is right, Manju is gone, you must accept it." Kaki flew into a fit and through her body from Ba and tried to grab Rekha. The women in the room, as if expecting this, surrounded her and two or three of them helped Ba hold Kaki onto the bed and tried to quiet her down. Rekha could not hold herself together anymore. She doubled over in her own pain of loss and cried uncontrollably.

"Oh…oh Manju, where are you? Someone bring my girl to me," Kaki cried out.

Through her flooded eyes and moaning she watched fascinated as she saw the women give Kaki some brown golden liquid with some white powder mixed in brandy – a dosage of opium, which took a minute quiet her down. Ba looked up, from her administrations, glanced at Rekha. *Was that sympathy? Was that compassion in her mother's eyes? Maybe she was just seeing things…*

"*Ja*, go now and check on your sister and the baby," she gently urged her daughter, "and then bring some *pani* and glasses for these ladies, it is getting hot in here."

The endless wailing from the women was both terrifying and irritating to her, they gave abandon to the sorrow, which was long and loud. For Rekha, this experience of death was the first in her family and did not know that this was necessary and expected. The men were quiet, standing outside in small groups, letting the women do the grieving for them.

Rekha left the room, relieved she did not have to witness anymore of this intense sorrow and had something to do, other than watch everyone cry around her.

She found Jyoti sitting with the other women in the kitchen and checked on both her and the baby. Jyoti's eyes were swollen from crying, but she had a calm sad face. The baby was fast asleep amidst the noise and chaos happening around her. Rekha went about getting the glasses and filling a jug with water from the tap and another *auntie* helped her carry it back to the bedroom. She served everyone and left the remainder of the jug on the nightstand and went back to join her sister.

A few hours later, Manjuben's father and Bapoojee arrived at the house. They had come back from the hospital, filling out the paperwork and making arrangements for the funeral, which would happen within days. They looked exhausted and beaten. Bapoojee went into the bedroom to check on Manjuben's mother and the women. Rekha heard the moans of sorrow coming from her Kaki again, as her father relayed the hospital administration process.

"*Bhai*, please bring her back to me. My only daughter, so beautiful, so kind…this was a mistake, God made a mistake," pleaded Bhartikaki, hoping someone, the gods, any god would listen. Rekha turned from the sounds of Kaki crying and saw her uncle sitting at the kitchen table, with his head in his hands, his shoulders shaking as he cried softly, the sound muffled from his hands. Rekha had a difficult time looking at her uncle, but stood next to him, gripping a chair, not knowing what to do. Her uncle took a deep breath, wiped his face with his handkerchief, looked up and saw Rekha's face. Without a word spoken between them, he reached out and patted her hand. Again, she was unable to stop the tears from pouring down face.

"I know, my girl, I know," he soothed and gently patted her hand again and then wiped her face with his own tear-soaked handkerchief. Rekha held her sobs in but she could not stop her shoulders from shaking. Someone put an arm around her shoulders, it was her father, it gave her some strength and finally her shaking stopped. Jyoti and the baby joined Rekha and their father and they stood, quietly together crying, not seeing any relief or way out to end to this nightmare. The wedding was never to happen. The only daughter of this house was gone. That beautiful, kind young girl was gone. Never to become a woman. Never feel the love of a husband and the contentment and pride in having children. *How will we go on?* Rekha wondered. No one had that answer, for her or anyone in this family.

Chapter 11

The days that followed were a long drawn-out blur. The wedding outfits were forgotten and pushed away in the wardrobes, all the food and wedding preparations were forgotten and stuffed away in the cupboards where they could be not seen. The first few days the whole family, except for Bapoojee and the boys, who worked in the shop, spent all of their time at the Manjuben's house. The girls did their best helping out with the house. The endless stream of visitors was a good support but also exhausting for everyone. Every time a person or family who had just heard the sad news, had to come to pay their respects, which replayed the entire first day. Both Kaka and Bhartikaki had to relive that horrible morning, recounting the series of events that led up to the death of their beautiful and only daughter. For Rekha, it was even more painful to watch, quietly sitting and listening to the horrible details. And it seemed with every re-telling, more details were added. Rekha and Jyoti took turns looking after the baby while helping out in the house. They served out the savoury snacks and food that people brought, cleared up and washed the dishes and helped clean kitchen. There was a lot to do, every day. Even with death, there were chores to do.

Rekha and Jyoti, exhausted from another day of visitors, sat at their kitchen table enjoying a cup of warm *chaa* in the evening.

"That woman was so bad today. I don't like her. Why did she even come?" Jyoti asked as she dipped her biscuit in her *chaa* and eating it quickly before it fell apart into her cup.

"Yah, I know, she was so rude. She thinks she is something, just because her husband is a rich doctor," Rekha replied reaching for another biscuit.

Then they both heard it. Rekha's hand stopped as she was about to dip her biscuit in her tea.

The noise was coming from their parent's bedroom. They both stopped and listened to the quarrelling, not surprised, considering how tired they all were. Jyoti got up from the chair and moved into the hallway to hear what they could be arguing about. They had both noticed that Ba was not looking happy as they left their uncle's house this evening. She had remained tight-lipped all the way home and was curt with both of them when they stepped into the house. She barked at them to make *chaa* for the family and walked into her room to put already sleeping baby to bed. The girls assumed it was because they were all tired from the long day. Jyoti quickly sat down again because the door to their bedroom abruptly opened.

"It is wrong!" Ba shouted at their father, as she walked out of the room. "God will punish them for this!"

"God has done enough…you don't think they have been punished already!?" he shouted back in outrage. He followed their mother out the bedroom and into the kitchen. They faced each other, although Bapoojee towered over his wife. She stood firm with the back straight, ready for a battle. Ba was never known to back down in a battle, whether it was with Bapoojee or other members of the family and the community. Everyone knew she had a temper and would open her mouth, when she did not like what she saw or heard.

"I will not be a part of this…Oh *Bagvan*, how can they do this!?" Ba flashed her steely eyes at him and clasped her hands together to her heart and prayed to the air above her, in hopes of reaching the gods. "She has to be burned in the fire to be purified."

Both girls looked at each other with saucer eyes and eyebrows raised and then back to their parents waiting for clarification. The girls knew better than to ask questions when their parents argued. They knew that their mother would turn on them in an instant when she was riled up.

"Can't you understand that this was something that Manjuben talked about and wanted. You don't understand it, but that does not make it bad. My brother wants to do anything that will make his daughter happy, even if she is dead," he said with quiet conviction. He was looking at his two daughters now and they both heard and saw his heartbreak. He was imagining if this was happening to him and what would he do make things better. He, like his brother, their uncle, was reaching for the smallest thing to make themselves feel better about this situation. As men, they felt helpless, they could not grieve or at least show their grief. The men did things. They worked, paid for things, planned and accomplished things. They did not have time or ability to cry or moan over loss. This was so true of their family and most of the community. Men do not cry.

"In any case," he looked back at his wife, "this is not your concern. It is their business and they will do what they must. You know and you have known this for years that Manju was afraid of fire. Try to understand. And if you cannot understand, at least show them your support and respect. If you can't, then it would be better that you don't attend the burial tomorrow." Bapoojee finished quietly. He took a glass from the cupboard beside the sink and went to another cupboard and poured himself a fair amount of whiskey. Without looking at anyone, he walked back to their bedroom and quietly shut the door. The girls sat silently and stayed frozen to their seats as their mother stood in the middle of the kitchen, unable to decide what to do next. She was speechless, a complete rarity for her. She had her face down, so they could not decipher what she was thinking. Without a word, she walked to her bedroom and quietly shut the door behind her.

The girls quietly finished their tea and washed up the dishes and performed their nightly rituals for bed. They were curious to see what would happen to tomorrow. Not just at the funeral, but also how their mother would act.

It was the third day since Manjuben had passed away and it was the day she was to be buried. The whole family was up early, before the sun and rooster could interfere with their dreams. In the darkly lit kitchen, the girls made *chaa* and toast for the family, while Ba tended to the baby. So, their mother was going to the funeral, despite her protests. Bapoojee must have said something to her last night. She was more subdued than usual, dressed in her plain white cotton sari, she actually looked pretty Rekha noted. *Was it the sari, was it her quietness that made her look that way?*

People always talked about how she was such an attractive woman, people would say these things to the Rekha and Jyoti, but the girls never saw her that way. To them, she was just their angry mother who never had a smile for them. Of course, she had all the love in the world for her boys, but the girls were second best and did not deserve her affection and attention. They were to be trained and groomed for the best possible match in marriage and be competent in the kitchen. Nobody was ever going to complain to Ba that she didn't even teach her girls to cook and clean. Even this morning, she woke them up with a snap to voice and instructed them to wear their plainest dresses and to bring cardigans to keep out the morning chill.

After the sombre breakfast, they got into the car.

"Bapoojee?" Rekha asked in her softest voice, as they all climbed in the car, "how will Kaka and Kaki get to the cemetery? We don't have enough space for them."

"Don't worry about them my girl. The neighbour will take them in his *Kombi*. They will see us there," Bapoojee answered with tenderness. He smiled at the children to reassure them. He did not look at Ba or speak to her during the ride to the cemetery. The children were satisfied with his answer and rode quietly for the whole journey to the cemetery. They didn't know where they were going. This was all new to them. Rekha found out, years later, there was special area for the Indians to bury their dead. For a while they passed streets and homes that they recognised, even in the dark, but soon, they were on a dirt road they did not know. It was dark without street lights, only the headlights of the car provided a view of what was in front of them. As they drove, the night lifted slowly.

"Look Rekha, the sun is coming up," Jyoti whispered, nudging Rekha, they all turned to watch the first rays of the sun slowly making its way up. There was a slight haze in the sky, with a mix red and yellow of the dawn breaking through. The rising sun gave Rekha some comfort and she looked around. They were in the middle of nowhere, the landscape offered view of vast fields with the occasional tree and bushes. This area was completely unfamiliar to Rekha and her family, it was so far from home. They crossed some railways tracks and then the car slowed to an area which was fenced off. Nothing of particular interest was there. There were no signs or markings around or near the entrance of the burial grounds. Rekha noticed four other mounds, as they walked toward the spot where a deep rectangle hole, the burial spot with Manjuben's body already laying inside. Some of the community members stood quietly waiting. Not too many, partly because not everyone was invited to the burial and partly because some them felt the same way as Ba. Many, saw it as an affront, to what was understood as acceptable, that cremation was the proper and right way. Bapoojee and Ba went and stood next to Manjuben's parents. All the children from both families stood slightly back behind their parents, serving no functional purpose except as observers. Rekha stood transfixed, not able to take her eyes away from the body that lay wrapped in plain sheet at the bottom of the hole. Both Kaka and Kaki were quiet as the priest offered the prayers which protected and encouraged Manjuben's soul to leave the body journey back to where it came. Later Rekha learned that this was guaranteed at cremation, which forces the soul to leave the dead body. The priest finished with his prayers in Sanskrit and sprinkled holy water on the body and asked Kaka and Bapoojee to participate by offering final prayers and blessings for the body. Both Rekha and Jyoti stood a little back from the open hole in the ground, trying not to look down and see their cousin's body wrapped in plain white muslin. They took turns holding the baby, who was unusually fretful, not content with either of her sisters. Rekha understood the baby's discomfort, thinking that she was uncomfortable being at the funeral sight, or maybe expressing the feelings that all the children felt. Unlike the baby, they could not show their fear or discomfort. They rubbed her back, cooed to her, shushed when her voice raised a little too loud. Rekha watched her mother as the priest did the final *mantra* and *arti*. She noticed her mother's mouth was turned down in a frown, her lips pressed tightly together, but couldn't tell if it was from the sadness of the situation or from her disdain of the burial. Rekha noticed that Bapoojee kept his attention on his brother and the priest and kept his gaze away from his wife. They all joined in the final offering of soil to the body. Kaki was crying with her head down, holding the mound of soil tightly in her hand, while Ba offered what support she could by holding her sister-in-law's small frame and patting her back.

Kaka and Kaki were the final ones to throw soil on the body, they both stood together and held out their shaking hands to drop the soil. Kaki looked at her husband and then back to the body, her hand shaking at the morning sky.

"Why did you do this? What have I done to deserve this!?" she angrily demanded of the divine gods, shaking her fist of soil at the sky. "Have I not been faithful in my devotion, my fasting, my *pujas* every day!? This is what you leave me with? A body in the ground? My only daughter taken from me forever!?"

"Stop, you must stop this," Kaka spoke to her softly, pulling her hand down, opening her hand and letting the soil drop on the body. Ba stepped forward to help Kaka. The black workers at the cemetery began to cover the body with shovels of soil. Kaka and Ba struggled to hold Kaki back as she reached for the dead body in the ground, in an attempt to stop the workers.

"No, please don't do that," she begged the workers, "Don't cover her, she won't be able to breathe. Tell them to stop *Bhabi*," as she looked to sister-in-law with pleading tear-filled eyes. Ba took in her in her arms and they both cried.

"I can't. They need to do their work. Manju needs to rest, let her rest. Let us go home and we can visit her again," Ba softly replied, which somehow calmed Kaki a little as she sobbed on Ba's shoulder. Rekha and Jyoti were so shocked by the outburst from their aunt, bringing both to more tears. Naïve and young, they believed that they had no more tears to offer after these past few days of constant grieving. The baby, now in Jyoti's arms, joined in the sorrow. The girls were also surprised that their mother had the ability to be so kind and gentle. This was a side of her they never knew existed. All of the women instinctively moved together in a small group, crying to each other and for each other, in grief and pain. The men and the boys stood by quietly and listened, awkward in their inability to show emotion or offer any comfort. Bapoojee offered his brother an arm over his shoulders for just a moment before moving to the women and girls and urging them toward the cars. Kaki was quiet now, still clinging to Ba. Bapoojee decided to put them and the girls in his car and Kaka and the rest of the family would come with the other cars that had come that morning. Rekha took one last look to the grave site. The workers were almost done now. It was then that Rekha realised that she would never see or hear her beautiful Manjuben ever again. Her heart gave a sudden jolt, like it was being squeezed from an invisible hand. She rubbed her chest with her hand, desperately trying to ease the pain. All through the long ride home, it did not relent. Rekha looked out the window, trying not to hear her aunt crying in the front with her mother. When they got to Kaka's house, Ba took Kaki inside, who was now limp with exhaustion and silent. Without a fuss, Kaki let her sister-in-law wash her hands from the last traces of soil from the burial. Ba took off Kaki's white mourning sari and left her in her petticoat and blouse and put on a warm soft cardigan for her. Ba beckoned Rekha, who stood at the doorway of the bedroom, to help her put Kaki to bed. Ba offered Kaki drink a short glass full of brandy, who took it without any resistance. She grimaced and coughed at the strong taste of the alcohol and finished it at Ba's insistence. Rekha and her mother both sat on either side of the bed, Ba stroking Kaki's head, as they waited for Kaki to fall asleep.

"Rest now, you need to rest," Ba softly crooned to Kaki. Rekha could not look at her mother, but instead gazed at her Kaki, who slowly closed her eyes and finally rested. Finally! She was free from her heartbreak for a few hours. Rekha desperately wanted to look at her mother, and see her face, but was too frightened. She wanted to see what her mother looked like. She knew it was silly to think so, but maybe, Ba would actually look like a kind mother. The kind and gentle mother she and her sister had always wanted. *Who was this person?* Rekha wondered to herself…she had so many questions to ask her mother, but remained silent, just listening to the sound of her mother's crooning. All of the events of the last few days were crashing down on her. She desperately wanted to run away and hide from it all, but there was nowhere to hide. There was no hope or happiness in sight for her. And there would never be any happiness for Manjuben.

Chapter 12

The next day, Rekha woke up with a start. The light was shining through the small window and the thin lace patterned curtains. She realised that both she and Jyoti had not woken up on time, in fact, they should've woken a while ago and it was late for them. Neither the birds nor the rooster had woken them up this morning. She lay on the bed, rubbing her eyes, and took a moment to remember what day it was, so she could remember what chores had to be done for the day. And then, she remembered! She remembered the whole week. The shocking days of Manjuben's death, the prayers and grieving, the funeral yesterday. Her shoulders slumped, feeling the full impact of what had passed. The realisation that her uncle and aunt and her family were left with the endless grief, the empty hole in their hearts hoping, in vain, that something would take away their pain. Rekha turned to her sister in bed and shook her shoulder.

"Get up!" she whispered to her sister, "We slept in!"

"What? How? What are you talking about? How could we have slept in?" Jyoti jack-knifed from her waist up with eyes wide open, still confused.

"Where is Ba? I didn't hear her shout at us? Did she call us?" she asked with surprise and confusion.

"No, she didn't and I don't know why. I didn't hear the rooster," Rekha replied softly in confusion, "I must have been so tired."

In unison, they scrambled out of bed and rushed for the door of their bedroom, opening it with caution, expecting something like a hurricane blow through the door. They stood silently and listened. They heard their father and mother in the kitchen. They walked down the hall and entered the kitchen and were little taken aback. Their parents were sitting at the table, talking quietly. The baby slept soundly in their father's arm, while he drank his chaa. He noticed the two girls standing by the doorway. Both silent and staring at their parents and wondering what to think of the scene before them.

He smiled and beckoned them. "Come my girls, did you wash your faces? Never mind, come and sit with us and have some *chaa* your Ba made. You can wash later."

The girls gave each other a look of shock, with highbrows raised and then smiled back at their father. But still wondering if there was trick involved.

"Jee Bapoojee," they almost replied in unison, making them both giggle quietly into their hands and they slowly approached the table. Ba pushed her chair back from the table and got up. Rekha and Jyoti stopped in their tracks, wary and watchful of what was to happen. *Why was she getting up? Was she upset with them now for giggling? Please don't ruin the moment*, Rekha pleaded to whatever gods were listening. But Ba simply got up to take some *bekkers* from the cupboard and poured the *chaa* from the simmering pot from the black stove, using a small tea strainer to clear the tea leaves into two small metal bekkers.

Ba set the metal mugs before the girls and refilled the plate of biscuits and the bowl of *chevro* for them as well. There was still a couple of pieces of toast on the plate that Bapoojee had not eaten yet. Rekha, trying to hide her shock and delight at being served by their mother, tried to remember the last time Ba had put a *chaa* on the table for her or her sister. Ba usually reserved such luxurious treatment for the boys, making the girls help her spoil the boys as much as possible.

"Eat, my *dikris*, take some toast and biscuits…you must both be hungry," Bapoojee urged, "we had a very trying week, full of misery and exhaustion. We must also to take care of ourselves too, you know."

They ate and drank with such pleasure, basking in the attention not normally afforded to the girls of this family. They smiled to each other a little, both happy and nervous as to what brought this on. But they took a moment and knew immediately that Ba and Bapoojee were thinking of their uncle and aunt who had just lost their one and only daughter to a senseless accident.

"Now girls, your mother and I were thinking that it would be nice if we kept an eye out for Kaka and Kaki once in a while. And you know how busy I am with the shop and your Ba is busy with the cooking and the house and you all…well. Let's see how I can say this…" he paused. Thinking of how to come up with the right words, without upsetting them too much.

"Your Ba and I would like you both to take turns sleeping one night a week with your Kaka and Kaki." He looked at them, expecting some kind of negative response from them. Although both girls had a look of surprise on their faces, it was so hard not to be happy at this opportunity. The girls looked at each other to confirm that they were hearing the same thing and it was actually true. But Rekha, after years of psychological abuse from her mother, hid her joy behind a solemn, straight face. She gave Jyoti a quick nudge under the table with her foot. Jyoti, until she received the warning from her sister, was beaming at her father with an open grin.

"Remember, I don't want the housework to fall behind, just because you will be going there now." Ba's quiet voice was unusual but a definite reminder that she was still going to keep them on a tight leash and she would not let them get away with anything. Jyoti's face changed quickly, the smile gone and replaced with closed mouth and she eyes looking down at her mug of tea.

"Jee Ba," the girls answered, again, in unison without hesitation. Both hearing the unspoken warning from their mother.

Ba sat down with them with a fresh mug of *chaa* for her and Bapoojee. They exchanged a few comments and questions about what was to happen for the grieving family. Ba did not speak to the girls, but sat silent for a little while. She then got up again, startling the girls, and walked to around Bapoojee. Both Rekha and Jyoti stiffened and stayed still as she walked behind them, again, waiting for something unpleasant to happen.

"Give her to me, her nappy must be so wet, wet, wet by now." She took the sleeping baby from her husband's arms and walked to the bedrooms. She stopped and turned around and looked at two daughters. They looked back at their mother and waited, Jyoti still holding a biscuit to her mouth, not knowing whether to put it down on her plate or eat it. They expected the worse, some kind of burst of anger or insult or threat…it changed in form sometimes, but the venom and malice never changed. Rekha and Jyoti had always spoke in hushed tones at night, to each other, about their mother and her volatile 'behaviour'. They wondered and tried to figure out why Ba was always so angry, and that anger was always directed to them and no one else. Jyoti finally took a quick bite of her biscuit, since it was melting and did not want to be scolded for wasting or making a mess.

"Now, make sure you clean up the dishes and pot after you eat. And remember to wash yourselves, there are a lot of chores to be done today. This house has been left to look like a garbage heap the last few days," Ba informed Rekha and Jyoti with a hard look. She turned and walked to her bedroom to change the baby's nappy and put her down for a nap. The girls looked to their father in shock, at being given a 'gentle' reminder about housework. *Who was that woman?* Rekha wondered the second time, in a short space of days. Until now, Ba was predictable, always grumpy and gruff and never a kind word to her daughters. They only heard sternness in her voice when she spoke to Rekha and Jyoti. The somewhat soft voice, less harsh than usual, they had just heard was always reserved for the boys and the baby. Rekha thought, *she must be putting it on for Bapoojee. Why else?*

"So, my girls…have you eaten enough? There is more *chaa*, your mother made plenty for all of us. Even for when the boys wake up," he inquired with a smile.

Rekha looked at Bapoojee and suddenly her eyes welled up. It was too much! The love and concern were too much and too soon after losing Manjuben. All the sorrow and grief came flooding back. Rekha could not face her father, her throat tightening with emotion and then finally the tears rolled down her cheeks. Jyoti took one look at her sister and she also joined in the crying, also remembering the ordeal they all just gone through.

"Now, now girls. Don't cry. It is over and she is resting in a good place. We must not cry too much and try to help Kaka and Kaki. You know your Ba and I were just talking about how brave you both were the past few days and realised how lucky we are to have two special girls," Bapoojee said with pride and tenderness. Hearing such tender words brought more tears pouring out. Both Rekha and Jyoti, hearing the sincerity of his voice and realising that their parents did love them, never ever hearing those words before. Indian families, especially this Indian family, did not have time for affection and praise for the female children. They cried even more, with their shoulders shaking and their tears fell on to their plates. Jyoti covered her face with both her hands trying to stop the flood of saltwater on her face, but it didn't help much.

"Come now, you must stop. It is not healthy to cry so much…you will get a headache. As you heard your Ba, there is a lot of work to do today. I must tend to some paperwork in the shop." Bapoojee got up and left the room. The girls, hearing the words of 'your Ba' and 'housework,' quickly recovered from their crying. That was something they could recognise and knew how to do, and do it well. Housework, there was always housework. No matter how bad life was and how sick or unhappy one could be, there was always housework, the daily details and chores of life that offered a sense of rhyme and routine that was comfortable and familiar. Rekha and Jyoti, instinctively and with familiarity, worked together to cleared up the mess, set up the table for the boys who would wake soon, and washed and dried the dishes. They moved to the bathroom to wash their faces and brush their teeth, taking turns spitting into the sink and brushing. They made their bed and changed into their regular work/cleaning clothes, ready the day's work ahead. Things may had changed for their family and for their uncle and aunt, but life went on. Bapoojee had to work in the shop still, Ba had to cook and clean and look after her children and her husband. Rekha felt so much pain at the loss of Manjuben, she just wanted to crawl into bed and sleep. *I am so tired*, Rekha whined to herself, *my head and my eyes hurt from all the crying...will this ever get better? Will this ever end?* Rekha wondered. She wished that she could just stop the clock on the wall for a few days. Just a few days, to catch her breath, regain her strength, if that was even possible. But she knew, time would not stop for them. They had to keep going and doing what was needed to be done.

Chapter 13

The days of grief rolled into weeks, which quickly turned into months and then it was already two years since the passing of her dear cousin. The summer months of December and January had passed quietly, except for the occasional thunderstorm that brought the much-needed water for all wildlife and fauna, but soon it would be fall and then winter. Although short, the winter months were intolerable for everyone. There was never a shortage of complaining about the cold. Thankfully, the African sun provided enough sunshine through the day, but that did not satisfy anyone. Just like Rekha's family, everyone sat in their kitchens where the black stove would provide warmth for hours. When it was time to go to bed, everyone would took a hot water bottle with them. Heavy blankets and other bodies that shared their beds, kept the heat in the beds. The pain of losing Manjuben had turned into a dull ache, rather than the intense biting pain Rekha had in her heart. Some memories were sharper than other but mostly viewed through a pink misty haze, like a beautiful sunset, seen only by her in her head, replaying the best moments they shared together. Sitting in their bedrooms, giggling about silly girl things. Standing next to each other at the kitchen while helping each other out in each other's houses. Enjoying the few weddings they had attended together and the last event they were together celebrating her upcoming wedding at the evening *Sangeet Garba*. The sweetest memory for Rekha was when Manjuben had spoken to her about her recent engagement to Bharat and helping cope with the reality of one day getting married and being a wife and mother.

Life for Rekha did not change much; the continual routine of cooking, cleaning and looking after her baby sister, who was now three years old. Until recently, her family spent time with the grieving parents almost bi-weekly. They had tried to keep both their Kaka and Kaki occupied, hoping to not let them feel left completely without anyone. Even Manjuben's brothers looked lost at times. The girls took turns staying with their Kaki one night a week each, helping her with the household chores, cooking a family meal, sitting with their uncle and aunt. They listened to stories about Manjuben when she a baby, or when she first walked, her first day at school when she cried so much at leaving her parents, that she vomited and had to be sent home. Sometimes, they laughed at the stories, but mostly they sat quietly together and remembered. Each, cherishing their own memory of her. At first, those evenings spent with Kaka and Kaki were difficult, especially for Jyoti. She usually came home the next day, going straight to school from their uncle's house and returning in the early afternoon. But she seemed more quiet than usual, less chatty about what happened at school or the uncle's house. Slowly, she decreased the time she spent there, mostly because she had so much homework to do, after coming home and helping Rekha with the chores. And then she complained she could not give Kaka and Kaki the attention they deserved when she was studying. They both worked extra hard and fast, so they could fulfil their parents' wishes to stay with their uncle and aunt. But in the past year now, it was just Rekha who went once a week, she usually ate the last meal of the day with them and then slept there. Both Babookaka and Bhartikaki looked forward to the visits. Kaki would make an extra effort, making their favourites for the supper – basmati rice and *masoor dhal* with potato fry or salt and pepper chicken – basic simple dishes, but favourites nonetheless. Rekha secretly thought Kaki was a much better cook than her mother. But God forbid if anyone, especially her, brought up that comparison. Ba always took pride in her food and pastries, too much pride. Ba, of course, was a good cook, and everything she made tasted good. But to Ba, any compliment to someone else's cooking was an insult to her. Jyoti and Rekha secretly agreed that their aunt was the best cook and never spoke of it in the home. The best part of this new routine was when Kaka would come home from the shop, he would bring a treat – a sweet candy or a chocolate. In the beginning, he would quietly put it in front of their plate as they ate their supper. Later, he made them guess which pocket of his suit contained the treat and then they would have to guess what it was. Rekha became the best guesser and Kaka finally stopped playing the game and would just leave it on the table for her. Rekha would always save it and share it with her sister the next day. Kaka, who had always been the jolly soul of the family, was quieter these days and didn't tell his silly jokes or long stories, that Rekha now suspected, were completely made up. His stories had been so full of detail in people, colour and drama. Rekha used to believe every single word he spoke. The older, more mature Rekha remembered his complex, fanciful stories and realised how much she actually missed them. He would now spend time, sitting quietly in the corner, listening to the radio or reading a book, more religious than before. *Looking for an answer to his question of why? Why did it happen to him and his daughter? What reason or sin committed in a past life would have caused such a horrible thing to happen to his family?* Things were never going to be the same and they all knew life had to go on.

Rekha also noticed a change in her family. Bapoojee was not as jovial as before and was more subdued when his brother and wife were around. He downplayed any family activity or tried not to bring too much attention to the girls, especially Jyoti's schooling and Rekha's eventual wedding. When they were not around, Bapoojee gave more attention to the girls. Ba was about the same if not worse. Rekha was still expected to do the same chores as before and complete any chores that Jyoti could not manage because Jyoti had to finish schoolwork. These days when Rekha went to her uncle's house, Ba seemed more angry and barely kept a civil attitude toward to Rekha. Ba was very curt and sharp in her instructions to Rekha, especially when no one was around. Even today, Rekha remembered, as she walked to her uncle's house, how Ba had showed her 'claws' and Rekha's face was still stinging from the slap. Rekha, as usual, rushed through her chores so Ba would not have anything to complain about before she left the house, to spend the night at Babookaka's house. It had happened after lunch. Bapoojee had returned quickly to the shops, complaining that today was a busy today and did not want to leave Kaka and the 'shop boys'-the two young black men employed at a menial wage, to do all the manual labour in the shop. They cleaned, carried, pulled, organised, dusted, delivered and basically carried the heavy load for Bapoojee and Kaka.

So Bapoojee rushed off to work. Ba finished her meal and put her plate and *bekker* to be washed by the sink and went to check on the baby napping in her bedroom. Rekha started washing the dishes after clearing up all the table. Her eyes were checking the clock, mindful the rest of things to be done before she could leave. She washed the dishes, dried the dishes, put away the dishes, prepared and cleaned the vegetables for the evening meal and washed the rice and made the dough for the *rotis*. Ba would make the rest of the meal and then Jyoti would help when she returned from school to make the rotis. Rekha silently continued her schedule and timeline for herself in head and she then suddenly froze. She realised that her mother had not gone to her bedroom but was standing by the doorway watching her. She turned and looked at her mother, waiting. Not completely sure what she would say or what was to happen.

"Well, you seem to have so much time, standing there daydreaming about what? Your wonderful evening with your Kaka and Kaki? Aren't you tired of spending time with them? Aren't you bored with their stories?" Ba asked in a taunting tone. "Well? What have you got to say?"

"No Ba, it is fine. They are just lonely...they miss Manjuben," Rekha answered quietly.

"Of course, they miss Manju, what a stupid thing to say!" she countered.

"Well, listen to me girl. You are not leaving this house until you clean the washroom. I want the shower stall, the toilet and sink shiny and clean. It is filthy and I want to take a nice bath tonight, before I sleep," she commanded.

"Jee Ba. I will clean it all before I go."

"It better be cleaned or else…" she finished her threat with a smile and walked away.

Rekha did not realise how terrified she was, until she realised her armpits were wet with perspiration. She would have to change her blouse before she left but after she cleaned the washroom.

As she bent over to clean the toilet and the floor around it, her thoughts wandered, as they did a lot these days about Bharat and her future. Her imagination went to fantasies of how she would, after she got married. She would cook sumptuous meals to please her handsome husband. Afterward, they would go out for long walks and maybe even go to the *Bioscope*-movies to see the latest Hindi film. Living in a big house with fancy furniture and modern appliances and maids for cleaning and for looking after her beautiful children.

"Aren't you done yet?" Ba shouted from her room, startling Rekha out of her daydream.

"Jee Ba. I am finished," she shouted back. She quickly got up, put the rags and soap away under the sink and rushed to her room to change her blouse. She did a final check in the mirror to fix her plaits and check her face for dirt or sweat, and walked out of her bedroom.

She saw Ba was standing in the kitchen and stopped. Ba had a gleam in her eye and showing a tight tense smile. It was the kind of look that was usually followed by some kind of abuse. Rekha was immediately frightened and worried, looking to see who else was around. To her dismay, there was no one about. Bapoojee was still in the shop. The boys and Jyoti were also in the shop.

"I see you are ready to go. That was quick, wasn't it?" Ba asked slowly.

"But I am finished. I cleaned the washroom," Rekha countered swiftly.

"Well then...show me." Ba moved toward Rekha with such speed and strength, as she grabbed her upper arm and pulled her toward the washroom. Rekha did not struggle, in fact, she was limp with fear, wondering what she had done now? Ba jerked her arm and made Rekha's head snap and her plaits swing around her head.

"Look at this! You think you are finished and done?" Ba demanded, pointing to the area around the toilet.

Rekha tried to remain calm and strained to find what she had missed. And then she noticed it. She had left a dirty rag behind the toilet. She must have missed it when Ba had shouted at her to finish.

"Well, explain yourself! Is this how I taught you to clean? What would people think if I sent to your in-laws today? How can I hold up my head, if you cannot even do a simple thing like cleaning the toilet? Hey!?" Ba shrieked at Rekha with her face right in her daughter's. Ba's eyes were wide with rage and spittle escaped her mouth as she shouted at Rekha.

"I-I am sorry," Rekha stammered out.

"You should be sorry, you good-for-nothing girl!" Ba sneered at Rekha as her eyes narrowed with menace and her face was ugly and full of anger. Ba pulled her out of the bathroom, with a tight grip, hurting Rekha's arm. Rekha closed her eyes in fear and helplessness.

"Look at me when I am talking to you! You stupid girl!" she shrilled and pulled Rekha's one plait, startling Rekha into opening her eyes. And then she heard it before she felt it.

The smack to her cheek came fast and hard. Her eyes flew open more in shock and she covered her other cheek with her free hand to protect herself, waiting for the next smack.

"Get out now, before I lose my temper completely," she hissed and pushed Rekha back.

"J-J-Jee Ba," Rekha stuttered quietly in reply. With her head down, she moved quickly to her room and picked up her overnight clothes and put on her old jersey cardigan. Ba stood there in the hallway watching her, with eyes lit with red rage. Rekha slinked past her mother, pressing her back to the wall, hoping she did not receive another blow.

"Yah…just go to their house. You think you are so special, don't you? Your head is getting bigger every time you go. Just you wait…one day, you will have a husband and children and in-laws too! See how happy you will be then! I hope I am alive to see what a big head you will have then!" she ranted, as she followed Rekha through the kitchen and to the door.

Rekha moved her feet, as quickly as she could, without actually running to her Bhartikaki's house. Rekha rubbed her face where the smack had landed, in an attempt to remove the pain and any mark that might have resulted from her mother's hand. She didn't realise that no amount of rubbing would stop her face from burning. She was determined that this incident would not ruin her time at Kaka's and Kaki's house and put on a smile as she entered the house. Thankfully the kitchen was not too bright, they only had one light on and rest of the light streamed in from the hallway. Her eyes brightened and her heart warmed a little when she saw the deep smile from Kaki's kind face, greeting her in the kitchen. She was pouring *chaa* into two pretty teacups, know that Rekha would arrive any minute. Babookaka, like her father, liked to sit with his short glass of whiskey. They both claimed with absolute certainty that the whiskey was good for them and helped them sleep better. Knowing how hard the brothers worked in the shop, both wives did not begrudge them this small thing.

"Come, *dikri*. You came just in time. Sit, I will bring some biscuits." Bhartikaki motioned for Rekha to sit on the nearest chair next to her. Rekha, sat opposite her at the table, careful not to sit too close. She quickly put her hand on her cheek, looking like she was pensive and lost in thought. Rekha remained silent for the night, trying as much as possible to look calm and contented.

"Do you need more sugar, Rekha? You are not drinking your tea," Bhartikaki asked.

"Oh no, Kaki, it is fine. I am just waiting for it to cool. Do you have any *rusks*?" Rekha asked, hoping to keep her aunt busy with other things so she did not look too closely or long at her face.

"Of course, let me get some for you." She went to the cupboard and pulled out the tin and placed it on the table in front of Rekha. "I should have taken them out earlier. I know how much you like them," Kaki commented with a smile.

She thanked her aunt for the *rusks* and looked happy busy dunking and munching, on the *rusks*, with her tea. But inside, her mind was swirling of questions she couldn't answer, her stomach churned with resentment and humiliation at the treatment she had just received from her mother. She was slightly irritated at herself thinking... *Why do I still get so upset? I should not be surprised. I should expect this treatment by now!* For a while, she listened to her uncle's stories from the shop. She nodded and smiled at the right times. Bhartikaki finished her tea and started preparing for the night and putting away the little things that were left behind by the boys who gone to their room, to get some reading in before they fell asleep. These cousins, unlike her brothers, loved their books. Rekha tried her hardest to listen to her uncle but she kept hearing a noise, it almost felt like a shout and at other times, it was a low keening noise, coming from her head. She didn't understand what it was, putting it down to mental tiredness or a headache.

"Kaki, if it is alright, I am going to bed now. I am tired from the busy day," Rekha asked, feigning a yawn and covering her mouth for extra show.

"Of course, my girl, you know where everything is, go sleep now. I will wash up." Bhartikaki smiled and got up to wash the last few dishes. Both her uncle and aunt smiled and said their 'good nights' to Rekha as she headed to the bedrooms. What she did not see was their look of concern for her. Babookaka shook his head and returned his attention back to his whiskey. They remained silent, lost in their thoughts.

Rekha walked away, hoping she did not bring too much attention to herself. Her pain in her head persisted but she knew it really wasn't a headache. It was something deeper than that. She didn't quite understand, but knew that it was her heartbreak. All the years of mental and physical pain she had endured had been pushed back through wall after wall. To survive she had constructed mental walls and pushed the pain away far back in her mind. This pain was attempting to surface, like a pot on the black stove, full of water and ready to bubble and spill over. Normally, she was able to keep this part of her well-hidden and under control. Lately, especially when she came to spend the nights with Manjuben's family, it seemed to surface more often. *Why here*? Rekha asked herself. As she lay her head down on Manjuben's pillow, many of the thoughts and questions she dared not think about at home poured out, like a broken faucet. *Why wasn't her mother like Kaki? Why was her mother so angry all the time? Why couldn't she had been born in this family instead or better yet…why can't she just leave her parents' house and move into this house? With this family, who liked her and treated her so nicely. But she knew better. She knew that nothing was going change until she got married, left her family and lived with her husband. But when would ever happen? How much longer do I have to endure and wait?*

Chapter 14

By morning, all her frustration and resentment were gone and Rekha woke up, refreshed with a smile on her face and in her heart. Her 'headache' was long gone and she woke up realising she was not in her own bed or her own house! She was still at her Kaka's and Kaki's house. Thrilled at the prospect of having breakfast with them before walking back with her uncle to the shop and her house, she walked straight into the kitchen to help out with breakfast preparations. The boys would be up soon too, waiting for their first meal. As she approached the kitchen entrance, she overheard them speaking of Manjuben.

"Remember how she used to insist on making *chaa* for us in bed on Sundays," Babookaka softly asked his wife, reminiscing about their sweet daughter. Bhartikaki, just nodded while quietly and deftly pouring the *chaa* into the teacups while balancing the steel tea strainer over the three cups in front of her. She had already put on her housecoat over her sari, ready for a day of cleaning and cooking. Kaka was dressed for work, with his face washed and hair combed down and heavily creamed down to suppress the few curls he had on the sides of his head. He had started to lose his hair and the hairline moved back with the increase of white hairs, as the months passed. He realised someone was in the kitchen and looked up with a ready smile.

"*Dikri*, you are up already? Wait, what is that on your face?" his smile disappeared, "What happened?" he questioned her with concern, his eyes trying to focus on her face.

"My girl, what has happened?" Kaki quickly put down the pot of *chaa* and strainer on the stove and moved toward her and inspecting her face.

"Kaki…there is nothing. I am fine," she replied. Rekha looked at both of them, confused as to why they were looking at her as if she had a giant pimple on her face.

"Who did that to you…oh my poor child, was it one of your brothers!? Was it accident or did they do it on purpose?" Kaki asked.

"I will speak to your father about this today!" Kaka vehemently declared.

Rekha was still confused and scared when she touched her cheek and realised it was slightly swollen and tender.

"Really, I am fine. They didn't do anything," she tried to reassure them again with one hand covering her bruised cheek and the other waving side to side in denial.

Kaki retrieved some *Zam-Buk*, from the small drawer used for the family medicinal items, a menthol salve remedy used for all physical skin ailments, bruises and muscle aches, bites and pimples. She walked to Rekha and took her hand covering the cheek and bent over to look closely at Rekha's face.

"Don't worry *dikri*, let me put some *Zam-Buk* on. It is will help with the bruising and swelling and it will not look so bad in a little while." Kaki's fingers gently patted Rekha's face with the salve as she spoke.

"Who would do such a thing?" she muttered, more to herself than to Rekha. But they all knew the truth. They all knew that Rekha's mother had a temper. They had known that, when Rekha was 'ill' and she had not come out of her room for those awful days – a long time ago. Manjuben had been so distressed and had asked to see her every day, but was firmly told not to go in or visit again, should she 'catch' the same sickness.

Kaka and Kaki had suspected and after the two brothers had spoken, in a brief discussion; did not say anything to Rekha's mother or to their own children.

"This nonsense has to stop. Some people don't appreciate what they have." Babookaka shook his head, while intently staring at his tea. He couldn't look at Rekha. Both Kaki and Rekha looked at each other with eyes with emotions of pity for Rekha and anger at her mother. But neither spoke, fearful that verbally acknowledging the abuse would make it worse for everyone, particularly Rekha. So, instead nothing was said and Rekha quietly walked back to Manjuben's room to dress and brush her teeth for breakfast. She took a quick look in the mirror and did not realise until she saw the evidence of her bruise that her face looked that bad. She overheard her uncle and aunt speaking with hushed voices, in the kitchen, but she couldn't make out what they were saying. Of course, it was about Rekha's face and her mother.

She quickly washed and dressed, sat at the kitchen table to eat her toast and drink the *chaa* that Kaki had made fresh for her. Kaka went to his room and Kaki was busy getting things on the table for the boys who would wake soon. Nobody spoke, the silence was thick in the room, like wading through a pool of mud. Rekha's throat was tight and her stomach was doing turns, but she was determined to eat her breakfast and finish the *chaa* that Kaki made. And then it was time to go home. Kaka came out with his coat and hat on, ready to walk Rekha home before he headed to the shop.

"Ready to go *dikri*? I am sure it is going to be another busy day like yesterday... we must make a move now," Kaka said with a broad smile. Rekha knew he forcing himself to be happy, but he was clearly not happy.

"Okay *dikri*, go nicely and take care of yourself. Don't work so hard." Bhartikaki smoothed Rekha's hair and patted her back, as if to imprint some magical power of protection on her.

"Okay...bye Kaki and thank you for letting me stay again. I will come back soon," Rekha promised. She caught the quick eye contact between Kaka and Kaki, they were clearly speaking without uttering a word and it was a conversation of worry, concern and anger.

"Yes, you are always welcome to come back here anytime. You must know that," Kaki confirmed.

They left the house and Rekha walked along side Kaka, as he took long strides and moved very quickly. She tried to keep pace with him, as best as she could, but it took an extra skip or little run to catch up with him. He kept his eyes ahead, his arms swinging and he did not say a word. They finally reached her house and he walked straight in through the kitchen and to the entrance of the back of the shop. He had completely forgotten to say good-bye Rekha, as he normally did. He had walked past Ba, who stood at the black stove stirring the dhal she was preparing for lunch. She did not realise after until her brother-on-law walked through the shop entrance, that anyone had come in. But she did see her daughter, whose head was down, walking to her room trying not to be noticed by her mother. The swelling on her face had diminished from the salve Bhartikaki had applied, but there was still a faint mark on her cheek that anyone could see, if they looked closely at her face. Hopefully, by lunchtime, the mark would gone completely.

"Oh, you are back. Good. There is a lot of work to be done today," she tautly informed Rekha.

"Check on the baby and see if she needs a nappy change and then come back to the kitchen. You can finish preparing the lunch meal."

Rekha stopped in her tracks and answered with her back to her mother.

"Jee Ba, I will just go to the toilet first and then do everything," she replied with a heavy sigh.

"Hurry then, I don't have all day to wait, you know," Rekha's mother sternly replied while she furiously stirred her dhal.

Rekha went through the rest of the day doing all the chores ordered to be done by her mother. By early afternoon, Rekha had finished the dishes from the lunch they had just finished eating. Her brothers and Jyoti had also come home from school and ate. Jyoti and her stood together at the sink, one washing and the other drying the dishes and pots with the kitchen cloth. Their mother was in her bedroom, putting the baby down for a nap.

"How was your evening with Babookaki and Bhartikaki last night? I didn't come back from school early enough to see you, before you went yesterday. And Ba was in such a foul mood yesterday. She pinched me on my arm, so hard, it is still sore now. And just because I didn't finish sweeping the kitchen floor fast enough for her!" Jyoti complained in a hushed tone, so their mother did not hear them. If Ba heard them gossiping about her and talking about their Kaka or Kaki and Rekha's evenings, there would be hell to pay.

"Yes, she was very angry with me just before I left yesterday. She was shouting about something and then she…" Rekha hesitated.

"She what? Tell me what Ba did to you?" Jyoti asked anxiously. After the last horrible incident, Jyoti was worried all the time, that it would be repeated or worse, while she was at school.

"It was nothing…she, ah…she just smacked me on my face," Rekha admitted, remembering her mother's face, angry and bitter with spittle spewing from her mouth as she raged at Rekha.

"It hurt so much and Kaki and Kaki did not see anything when I arrived, but my face was puffy and bruised in the morning. They were not happy," Rekha recounted their reaction to her bruised face.

"What was she angry about now?" Jyoti questioned.

"It was the toilet. She did not like the way I cleaned it," Rekha explained.

"Oh God, why is she like that? Angry about little things like that. It doesn't make sense."

"And…and I think she doesn't like me going to their house anymore. She knows that I, that we, like going there," Rekha continued.

"I know, I know what she is like." Jyoti whispered in agreement, "That is why I stay home to do my homework. I thought that if I stayed home, it would make her feel better. You also need a break from her, being in the house all day with her."

As long as they could remember, Ba was an angry and jealous person. She disliked hearing about other people's happiness, joy and if they could make or do things better than her, particularly, if these people were her siblings or family, she felt even more resentful and angry. She truly believed she was the best at everything and had to be in control over everyone and right about everything. It was her way or no way! The girls learned very early to keep their small joys in life, or praise and admiration of others to themselves.

The girls finished the work in the kitchen and prepared themselves for bed. They got into bed, both quiet and pensive, looking up to the ceiling, lost in their thoughts. They felt a deep bond between each other, two sisters suffering from lack of love from their mother, but did not feel comfortable enough to show their love for each other. Their family, like many people and families in their culture, did not know how to express their feelings. But they were both aware, they were unhappy and fearful of how much more they would have to endure with their mother. Although they had 'good' comfortable lives with food, a home, siblings and a good father, they both knew there had to be something better for them. A better, happier life, somewhere with someone.

Rekha turned her body to face Jyoti and whispered to her sister, "Jyoti, let's make a promise to each other."

"Yes, yes, anything," Jyoti agreed and turned to Rekha and nodded happily.

"Let's promise that when we leave this family, we will have a good and happy life," Rekha said.

"Yes, I promise," Jyoti nodded with a huge smile on her face.

"And we must promise that we will be good and happy with our husbands and our children."

"Oh yes, I promise. But I wish that would happen tomorrow. I cannot wait for so long." Jyoti lamented and squeezed her eyes tight, trying in vain to make her wish come true.

"Yes, me too. I wish I was getting married tomorrow." Rekha sighed and yawned and turned onto her back, gazing at the ceiling, her eyelids heavy with sleep, hoping that tomorrow would bring all the answers to her dreams.

Chapter 15

At first, Rekha had waited for days for something happen, after the night Ba had slapped her. Those days turned into a fortnight and still nothing. Babookaka had been so angry and determined to say something to his brother. He was hoping to change what was happening in the house, especially to Rekha, who took the brunt of the abuse. She was the easy target being home all the time. Sadly, nothing changed and the abuse continued; Ba was more careful not to do anything that would show on Rekha's face. As Rekha grew older, the physical abuse waned and simmered down to taunting and berating. There weren't many slaps or pinches, but occasionally, it would just happen. Nowadays, Ba would use the spoon, or whatever was in her hand to hurt them. Jyoti was at home now. Ba had made such a fuss about her going to school. She badgered Bapoojee for days and wailed on about how she needed Jyoti at home to help with cleaning the house and cooking for her growing family. Ba would still pick on the girls, especially when they were alone, busy with their tasks and chores. So, some things had changed, but not everything. The visits to Kaka and Kaki had stopped by the end of that year. Rekha missed those evenings, left with nothing but happy memories to keep her company.

Time shuffled on, slow as molasses, and the daily routine never changed for Rekha, who was now a mature young woman at 16 years old. She was taller than her mother and almost reached her father's shoulders. Her face now resembled a full moon, with deep dark eyes with a high forehead, high and full round cheekbones and full lips. Her figure had filled out with full plump breasts and wide hips. Some would say that she was a little on the heavy side, while many men in the Indian community considered that shape very sensual and beautiful. Rekha did not see this or understand the attraction. She had no experience or exposure to any young boys, or men, except for the men in her family. For the most part, the girls were secluded from men of the community except when the men, as fathers or sons, came to the house to visit or when there was a function to attend in the community. But the girls were still never allowed to move very far from their mother's watchful eye, or any other woman's view in the community. There was an understanding that all the girls must be watched and protected, at all times. Rekha did not really understand why she and her sister and other young girls were kept controlled under such rigid boundaries. She only understood it as another form of control that their mother had on them. *Her mother did not want them to have fun and it was because of her that they did nothing and went nowhere!* Her mother never showed any interest in her or any of the women in the family. In her eyes, the girls were there for a purpose, which was to feed the family, clean the house and provide laundry service. Rekha knew this better than anyone. She also understood that she was now fully trained and did not have much more to learn from her mother. Like all women,

Rekha knew about housework. It was always there every morning, waiting, beckoning her every day as soon as she opened her eyes. By now, what she had once considered boring and difficult was now comfortable and familiar. She knew exactly what to do and when and did not to be told or reminded. She, like her mother, had an inner clock that started in the early morning hours and ticked the minutes and hours until every task that was needed to be completed that day, was completed. Jyoti, 13 years old now, was a little taller but looked the same as before, still thin-boned and angular, but with small breasts and no hips to show her initiation of womanhood that came later to her, than her sister. Rekha had started her 'monthlies' at the age of ten years old. Jyoti, unlike Rekha, had her sister to go to when she first noticed the flow of blood. Rekha had been reassuring, but very matter of fact about the whole thing. She gave Jyoti the same instructions about using the rags, and cleanliness, as was given to Rekha when she had started her 'monthlies'. Jyoti was the 'second in command' now after Rekha and they worked well together, reminding each other or covering the tasks that they each preferred to do. Jyoti liked doing most of the cooking, while Rekha liked to do the laundry which included, repairing and sewing of clothes. Jyoti had taken over the household duties and the daily cooking with the help of Rekha. She missed school terribly, but knew that any complaining would go to deaf ears. Instead, she took solace in knowing she had the company of her older sister. The 'ruling and dictates' of Ba could not be changed or broken.

Their younger sister, Rita, once a little baby, was now almost five years old, a good-natured child, with the typical

Indian dark hair and eyes. Her wild curly hair always in two little plaits coated in coconut oil. She was a smaller replica of her two older sisters, but took more after Rekha in the physical attributes, with pudgy arms, legs and face. She would be ready for school soon. She now slept with Rekha and Jyoti, and was squeezed in the middle between the two, in their double bed.

Ba had two more babies after Rita. Ramesh, who was three and half years old. He had slept with his parents in the small cot, but was squeezed in with the boys, when the newest addition to the family came. A pretty little baby girl, Lakshmi, who was reaching a full year old this month. She had been born too early, with a lot of problems. She had been sick for the earlier part of her first year. And she, more than all the other babies, needed constant looking after. She still did not sit up on her own. She needed to sit in someone's lap or be supported by a pillow or rolled blanket when left on the chesterfield or bed when she was awake. She could stand on her feet when supported, but could not move her feet to walk. She needed assistance with sitting up straight to eat and still drank from a glass nursing bottle. Her meals consisted of bread soaked in warm milk and spoon-fed to her, by Ba or the girls. Ba needed more time to get things done in the house now and provided whatever help she could for the shop. The shop was busier than ever these days, keeping the whole family occupied. Rekha could see that Ba was not as spry as she used to be. She moved a little slower and didn't rush like she used to.

No one, especially Bapoojee and Ba, in the family never spoke of it, but Rekha and Jyoti remembered well the night Lakshmi was born. It still made Rekha shiver to recall the horrible noises that came from their parent's bedroom that night and how worried their father had been. They had sat in their room together, quietly listening to the audible drama and tension as the evening worn on. They had heard flutter of footsteps coming and going into the room. They knew that Bhartikaki was in the room with another woman from the neighbourhood. She was a small dark Indian woman, who the girls knew would always show up for all the births – midwife to the Indian women in their community. The girls had never seen Bhartikaki so nervous and worried, who kept asking the midwife if everything was going to fine. They heard Kaki crooning to their mother at times, and at other times, encouraging her to keep strong and then chatting about nonsense, to keep them both occupied. But soon, the time between the long sharp pains quickened and with such fierceness, it happened faster than they had all anticipated. The girls were used to births, as all of the children were born in the house and knew what to expect and how to help. They had heard the grunts and groans coming from their mother, who had given birth to many babies. On the morning of that day, Ba had stayed in bed, which was unusual itself. But the girls knew her time was soon and she was probably tired from the days before, cleaning and fussing, as she always did, when she was about to deliver the baby. Ba did not have the patience of most pregnant women, in fact, she was the opposite, becoming more agitated and restless as the due date approached. The girls carried on with the daily routine, occasionally stopping in to check on their mother throughout the day. By afternoon tea-time, Rekha stepped into her mother's room with a metal *bekker* and some plain rusks to leave on the small table next to the bed. Ba laid on her bed, on her side and was slowing rubbing her baby bump. All day, Ba refused to eat but Rekha hoped that, at the least, she would drink her tea and eat a few rusks.

"Rekha, is that you?" Ba asked in a slow quiet voice, eyes shut.

"Jee Ba, I brought you some *chaa*," replied Rekha, moving around the bed to see her mother's face.

"I need you to tell Bapoojee to call your Kaki and the midwife. Hurry, do it now!" Ba implored and then, let out a groan of pain. Rekha took one look at her mother's face and knew it was time. Without a reply, Rekha left the *bekker* on the table and rushed to the shop to get her father. He saw the look of panic of Rekha's face and wasted no time to get the midwife. Kaka quickly served the last customer and closed the shop. He then rushed over to his house to get his wife. Both the girls did what they knew had to be done. Putting on a few pots of water for boiling, they gathered the clean towels and the rubbing alcohol and the sterilised the small sharp scissors Ba kept ready purposely, for the time when it came. Prior to the days and weeks when the baby was expected, Ba would repeatedly remind them of the cupboard of things needed for the birth, even though the girls knew where everything was kept.

But this time, their help was not needed and they were told to stay in their room by that midwife woman. The boys were sent to Kaka's house to sit with their cousins. Everyone called her the 'midwife or Auntie' the woman who was summoned for all the births in the community assisted by helpers, like family and female community members. The 'midwife' was an elderly woman, at least in her 40s or 50s, not really a nurse or medically trained person, but someone who had the most experience and knew about births and babies. Not much was known about her, but the women of the community had gossiped about her for years, putting together pieces of information. The most common believed version was that she was seeing a Muslim man, in the small town she came from, possibly Roodeport but not completely confirmed. Her brothers had found her and the Muslim man together and beat both of them. The Muslim man had been hurt so badly, he became blind and lost the use of his legs. He was bedridden for life and useless to any woman as a husband and earner. He could not help her. She was sent away to a distant cousin's house living near Johannesburg, to quell the scandal and keep the two lovers apart. Some say she was pregnant and gave birth to a dead baby. Others say, the baby was born alive and taken and quite possibly killed by her brothers. After a year, she had left that cousin's house in the early hours to escape. Some say she was abused by that cousin's husband but the woman was blamed – *it was always the woman's fault*. The midwife now moved from one Indian town to next, spending a few years at each place. Of course, no one would ask her directly what had really happened, because gossiping and spreading rumours was a favourite past time and everyone took part. *And who would believe her story?* Rekha had always wondered what had really happened to Auntie, because she was not the most beautiful woman, actually far from it. She was short and round, with a square face with a long pointy nose and a wide forehead, always furrowed, looking tense and worried. With all the babies she had delivered, no one had ever seen her smile or laugh. In fact, she never showed any emotion. *Who would fall in love with someone like that?*

But right now, that was not Rekha's problem. She was worried about her mother, the baby and her father who sat at the kitchen table with a glass of whiskey, head in the hands. Babookaka sat next to him, refilling the glass, eyes nervously watching the door, listening to the muffled groans, coming from the bedroom. At one point, both girls jumped up, one clutching her heart and the other ringing her hands, when they heard their mother utter a heart wrenching scream, something they had never heard their mother do before during childbirth. It was horrible, like someone had stabbed her with a sharp object, like a fire poker. The girls knew that their mother would never lose control of herself making such a noise, if she could help it. Their mother had always talked about and was very proud that she did not "make a nuisance of herself" like other women did, when giving birth. Ba always talked about how weak the women were, when they shouted and cried while giving birth. Ba would always retell the story of how in India, her mother and aunts would give birth while working the fields. They would continue working after the baby was born with the baby on their backs or the front of their bodies, tying them tight with their saris, so they could work on, until it was time to go home. Rekha and Jyoti would always marvel at these stories of India and how their parents lived. To Rekha, they were like super humans, or the gods and goddesses she had learned about in Gujarati school, divine beings able to do and endure anything.

"My God Rekha! What is going on?" Jyoti asked her sister, looking for an assuring answer, knowing that nobody but the midwife knew the answer. After some time, which felt like hours, they heard few low moans coming from the bedroom and then the faint crying of a baby. The door of their parent's bedroom opened, and Bhartikaki quickly moved past their room and headed to the kitchen to speak to her brother-in-law and get another big bowl of hot water as the midwife requested. The two sisters rushed to the kitchen to hear what happened.

"Ba is fine and the baby is a girl. She is also fine. But your mother is very weak and tired."

"And the baby, what happened? This was not like the other times, it took so long," asked Bapoojee anxiously.

"The baby looks fine but she came out with the cord around her neck. She was blue when she came out, but the midwife got her breathing alright now. The midwife is looking after *Bhabi* now." She assured him taking a deep breath and turned to the girls with a thin smile. The girls exhaled, not realising they were holding their breath and watched their father and uncle take another swallow of the whiskey.

"Let me just take this to the midwife." Bhartikaki turned with bowl of warm water in her hands.

"I want to see them now." Bapoojee smacked his glass on the table, quickly stood up and started toward his bedroom. Bhartikaki walked to him and blocked his way halfway in the hallway and pulled his sleeve with one free hand, as best as she could, to stop him for a moment.

"Yes, but…please let her rest. This one has taken a lot out of her," Bhartikaki spoke softly. She moved closer to him, hoping the girls did not hear her. He knew something was not right with this birth. He had to bend his head, as she was much smaller than his own wife, and listened as she whispered in his ear.

"She lost a lot of blood; the midwife is trying to stop the bleeding with her medicine. She said we have to watch both the baby and *Bhabi* for the next few days," she nervously informed him, with her eyes steady and checking over his shoulder, ensuring the girls were still in the kitchen, not able to hear her.

"*Bhai*, you must call the doctor to check *Bhabi* and the baby," she offered nervously, eyes cast down, not used to telling her brother-in-law what to do. He looked at her in shock, searching his sister-in-law's face for more information. But she held her head down in respect. It did not take him too long for him to realise, then, what she was trying to tell him – he might have lost his wife.

"Yes, you are right. I will send for the doctor first thing in the morning," he assured her with a pat on her shoulder and went into the darkened room to see his wife and child.

The doctor came the next day, examined the baby and Ba. He assured Bapoojee that the midwife did everything she could have done and gave instructions for Ba to rest in bed with the baby for at least two weeks. Ba stayed in bed for ten days, while Rekha and Jyoti did what they were expected and trained to do and took control of everything in the house. During the first week, Bhartikaki came, once in the day and once in the evening, to check on the baby and Ba and also to see how the girls were doing. She brought special food for Ba that was only for her. Traditionally, when a woman has her first child, she goes home to her parent's home, just before they expect the baby arrive to give birth and/or recover from the birth. Rekha always heard the women talk about this 'confinement' period, thinking it was some kind of special punishment that the husband's family did to get rid of the pregnant daughter-in-law because she was useless near her delivery time and could not do any heavy housework. But later, much later, she realised that the 'confinement' was actually a good thing, which allowed the new mother to rest and recover, to eat special food and traditional herbs made at home. Since Ba did not have any family in South Africa, she had to rely on her sister-in-law and the generosity of the neighbours. Bhartikaki also knew that since this was the ninth child and nobody would be running to help her sister-in-law, it was up to her to help the family. Bhartikaki brought something new each day to help heal Ba's body, restore her strength and to maintain a good milk supply for the baby like paaks traditional Indian herbs Taken like a sugar-coated pill. Ba would take in between and with each meal, as well as, healthy soups and broths. Each day, the girls were given instructions by Bhartikaki, as to what meals to cook that would ensure giving Ba the necessary vitamins and protein that would ensure Ba's recovery, while also avoiding giving the breast-fed baby too much gas. By the end of the week, Ba insisted on sitting at the kitchen table to drink her tea and eat her meals, but tired easily and went straight to bed after eating. No sharp commands or direction given to the girls. They knew what to do and she knew it. She left them to the running of the house and Rekha understood that Ba was more ill than ever before and was still not completely back to herself yet. The doctor had assured Bapoojee that she would be back to full strength by a fortnight. Jyoti had the taken over most of the caregiving of the younger ones and the new baby. Rekha made sure the meals were on the table on the right times, the laundry was washed and ironed. The boys helped by playing with the little ones when they came home from school, but they also had homework to finish. Everyone did their part. The first couple of weeks, even Bapoojee stayed home nights, not going out to drink or play cards with his brother and buddies, as was his usual routine a few times a week. He stayed home and sat with his wife in their bedroom or played with the little ones. He would spend his time reading the Johannesburg Star newspaper or listening to the radio, while he sat in the front room. But he always took a peek in the bedroom. Just having him around gave Rekha a deep assurance that things were going to fine and made her feel that she was able to handle any heavy responsibility placed on her shoulders. *Everything was going to be fine,* she promised herself, *just fine.*

Chapter 16

It was late April and winter was approaching again, with its crisp and dry air, bringing in a slight chill in the mornings and evenings. The hot water bottles were pulled out of the where they had been stored, unused all summer long. Those people who were not well-off, heated bricks on their stoves and covered with them old clothes and put them in their beds. The days and nights were shorter now, but for Rekha and her family, they flowed into one long blur of routine. Thankfully, there weren't too many visitors to gawk at their mother and the new baby, except for the steadfast Babookaka and Bhartikaki. This was a huge relief to Rekha and Jyoti, who never enjoyed the amount of work and pretence involved when visitors came. The girls learned early on, that most visitors came out of boredom. They needed some distraction or news they could gossip about and spread. Some members of the community were extremely good at this and made it their favourite past time. They would visit one home to the next home, collecting bits of information to share with the next family, inventing a morsel of intrigue to enhance the story for their own amusement. Unfortunately, the information that was shared was also accompanied with a tinge of judgment, resentment, envy or malice that made things more sad, horrific or unhappy than they really were. The Indian rumour mill of Johannesburg, in fact, South Africa was a well-oiled machine and never failed to surprise Rekha's parents and family. Bapoojee always said these people had idle hands and idle minds. If they put the same amount of energy to good hard work, they would accomplish so much and would not have so much free time to judge others. Even within months of Manjuben's passing away, rumours had reached Bapoojee's ears that people were talking about how Manjuben had killed herself, because she did was not happy with the boy and family she was getting married into. This piece of news, thankfully, did not come from a visitor to the house or a visitor to Kaka's house, but rather, it came from a customer in the shop from another small town. Nobody else knew why Bapoojee was so furious, that evening, as he ate his supper. The two younger ones had been fed early and put to bed. The older children and Ba knew something was not right at the supper table. Usually, he told stories about the customers and asked the children, mostly the boys, about their day/school events. But that evening, he ate quietly, with his head down. He did not speak to the children at all. While everyone ate, Ba went to her room to put the baby down for the night and the girls finished up and went about cleaning up after the meal. The boys were almost finished, eating slower than usual, a little frightened about their father and his dark mood. Abruptly, Bapoojee got up and washed his hands at the kitchen sink, took a clean short glass from the cupboard and then went to the other cupboard where he kept the whiskey. With bottle and glass in hand, he went straight into his bedroom and loudly shut the hard behind him. He had not spoken a word to any of the children. Rekha was quietly hurt, that he did not even spare a smile or a look to her the whole time. They all looked his way as he walked away from them and they all jumped at the sound of the door slamming. The boys sat with their mouths open, the one hand full of food about to be shovelled into their mouths. Then, all the children hear the rumbling of their father's voice. He was shouting all sorts of obscenities and vile names, but they weren't sure to whom. They knew Bapoojee never lost his temper or used such language, unless something was very wrong. They were certain their mother was not the target of his anger. Rekha heard bits and pieces of the ranting and tried to put them together, to determine what her father was shouting about. Usually he grumbled about the customers, the workers or the shop, and sometimes about Ba, who pushed him too far. And usually, this happened with a few drinks after dinner or after he returned home from his nights out. But not that night. Rekha was the only one brave enough to inch closer to the bedroom door to hear her parents better. The boys and Jyoti stood in the kitchen, in the area where the hallway opened to the kitchen. They were terrified to step any closer, but still inquisitive enough to wait to hear what Rekha could find out.

"Those bloody bastards! They think they are so much better than us. How can they make up such outrageous lies!?" Bapoojee railed in his room, "I have a good mind to go to those people and give them a good 'hiding' – I want to bash them in their face!" he threatened.

Rekha was shocked to hear her father speak with such anger and violence. The worst she ever heard was when her parents argued in their bedroom and that was when he had too much to drink with his buddies.

"Ssssh! The baby is sleeping now and you are making such a racket!" Ba hissed at him, "and what are you going on about?" his wife asked, as she put the baby in the bed, already wrapped in the thick blanket, surprised at his escalating anger.

"Today, a customer from another town came in and told me, people are saying that poor girl killed herself because she didn't like the boy," he quickly relayed the story.

"What!? How can they say that? It is nonsense! We all know how happy she was with the match," said Ba.

"Yes, exactly. They make my blood boil!" he whispered fiercely.

"Just leave it. You know if you make a fuss, Baboo and Bharti will find out. And then what will you do?" she questioned, "Have they not had their share of suffering?"

"But wait, that is not all. They are saying other things, horrible things," he added.

"What? How horrible could it be? The poor thing is gone and the parents have suffered some much," Ba countered.

"This man said people are talking. Talking about what that poor girl did and how she brought shame to the family. Her whole family, which includes us. People are saying that even our girls are not a good choice for marriage."

"No!" Rekha could hear the shock in her mother's voice. "You mean they are talking Rekha? How can they do that? What have we ever done to people, but help them? Where would they buy their things if we did not sell it for them!?" she challenged.

"I just want to stop them. To shut them up!" Bapoojee said.

"Who are you going to shut up? You don't even know the names of the people who are spreading this nonsense, except the stupid man who came into the shop." Ba challenged her husband, "Some bloody people have nothing better to do in their own lives, so they make up stories like this. But really you must calm down, there is nothing you can do right now." She assured him. "But you are right. We must do something about the gossip which will affect all of us. And we must do something soon." Ba put emphasis on the word "soon."

"Ya, ya, maybe you are right," he conceded. Rekha heard the tinkling of bottle to glass. Bapoojee was pouring himself another swig of whiskey. "But when and what?"

"We will talk about this more tomorrow. But for now, lie down and rest a little," Ba urged with a gentle firmness to her husband, "and please don't drink any more, you know what that does to your head the next day."

"Ya...but I will have to contact that boy's father and sort this business out as soon as possible," he sighed. "There is so much to do."

"Yes, there is a lot of work, but we can do it. Look how much we helped your brother. It can be done. Now, lie down and rest," Ba replied, with confidence and pride.

Rekha heard the springs of the bed creak and then the voices dwindled down to whispers until she could not hear much at all. Rekha grabbed her heart feeling the shock hit her chest, when she heard what her father told her mother. Her eyes immediately with water, filled with sadness at the pain she felt. She upset about the gossip about Manjuben.

How could people be so cruel? Didn't they know how happy Manjuben had been with her upcoming nuptials? She was so happy, she glowed! How these stupid people talk about her Manjuben like this? Stupid, stupid people! Rekha had the same urge as her father to just scream and shout at these people. But wait, what where they talking about doing 'something soon'. Were they talking about her? And the boy… it could only be Bharat.

Rekha was about to move away from the door, not wanting to hear anymore slander against her beloved Manjuben, when she heard her name being mentioned. She pressed her ear to the door, hoping to catch whatever she could. She was partly terrified that Ba was going to complain about her to Bapoojee. But this past year had been without too much harassment from Ba. Everyone was too busy with school, the shop, the household chores and looking after the little ones. She did hear her name, but they were talking too softly for her to catch anything. Rekha quietly backed up from the bedroom door, turned and walked back to the kitchen to tell her siblings what she had heard. She had a slight hesitation in telling them. She didn't how what to say, still trying to take in all that she had overheard. She stood facing her siblings who were waiting to hear. All were them were quiet but visibly tense, each suspecting they had done something to anger their father so much. She swallowed her anger and hurt about Manjuben. But more frightening and exciting at the same time, was the news about her and Bharat. She didn't know what to say or how to begin. She looked at their faces.

"Well…what is going on? What has made Bapoojee so upset?" Jyoti asked, the only one brave enough to question their sister. Rekha looked them and decided that she did not want this story repeated and to upset anyone else.

"Oh, you would not believe it. I heard him say something about some man, a salesman he knows, who came into the shop and tried to swindle Bapoojee and Babookaka out of the profits of some goods." She lied, making up whatever story she could think of at the top of her head.

"Really!?" the boys asked in unison, as they wiped their brows, physically relieving their tension. "He didn't say anything to us earlier."

"Is that all? He is that upset over the salesman. It sounds like something much worse," Jyoti enquired further. She wasn't convinced that their father would get so angry over the shop. He always maintained such control and was level-headed when it came to business matters.

"Well, to tell you the truth, the salesman also complained about how he was ill-treated by Babookaka in the shop. And this man called Kaka some bad names as he was getting thrown out of the shop," she added for a little spice.

"What did he say to Babookaka?" asked Arun, eager to hear some vile language coming out of Rekha's mouth.

"I don't know, I didn't hear that part. They were talking too softly for me to hear," Rekha replied.

"*Ack man*, you should try to listen more!" Jayesh insisted, clearly disappointed they had missed out a good shouting match.

"Are you sure, it was not something else?" Jyoti asked again. She and Rekha always shared everything and felt as if Rekha was holding something back.

"Of course, what do you think? That I am lying? If it was something any of you did, wouldn't I tell you to warn you that you were going to be punished?" Rekha asked with enough impatience in her voice, putting on a good show to make them believe her.

"No, no. Of course, you would tell us," Jyoti soothing Rekha.

"Good, now let's finish the rest of the cleaning up here and go to bed," Rekha instructed her siblings. They listened, not challenging in any way, partly out of relief that Bapoojee was not angry at any of them. They all quickly cleared up and went to their separate rooms, to change, with their individual hot water bottles and be ready for another day. Rekha was so relieved to see that her acting actually worked on them and she tried to hide her anxiousness as she and Jyoti prepared for bed. Her heart thumped loudly as she changed into her nightgown. Rekha took two deep breaths and pressed her closed fist to her chest to ease the erratic beating, but nothing worked. She snuck a look at sister to see if Jyoti had noticed anything. No, she was doing her usual chattering before bedtime. Some of it about school and some about Bapoojee's behaviour this evening. Rekha acknowledged her conversation with a murmur here and there. Luckily, Jyoti could carry on conversation with herself without too much exchange expected from Rekha. *What was going to happen now? Does this mean I will be married soon!? What else could Bapoojee have meant when he had said, "sort this business out..."* Rekha put her head down to the pillow with a huge smile on her face, squeezing into the bed, careful not to squash little Rita in the bed already. She moved her arms and legs straight so there was room for all three of them comfortably. Luckily, the room was dark now and Jyoti could not see how happy she was. Jyoti would question why Rekha was happy about Bapoojee being so angry. Pressing her heart with her hand, trying to stop the increasingly loud thudding, feeling the excitement building to a frenzy. It took her a long time to finally fall asleep that night. Hundreds of thoughts and images raced through her head about the soon to come wedding and wonderful life with her wonderful new husband. Jyoti had long gone to sleep but Rekha stayed up thinking and thinking some more. She had already forgotten about the horrible things people were saying about Manjuben. She was too busy thinking about all the preparations and arrangements that had to done, getting herself ready. *To be a married woman! But when?* Her eyes closed, heavy with images of her sitting in front front the wedding pyre with her husband-to-be sitting next to her and the sound of the priest's voice droning on with ancient Sanskrit verses. Flowers and rice flying through the air...finally being loved by someone.

Chapter 17

Almost a week had passed and Rekha's heart was singing with happiness. She woke early, springing up from bed, bright and awake. Her body tingling with anticipation of the 'news' that was to be revealed to her and the rest of the family. She lit the black stove, warming up the kitchen and brewing the tea for breakfast, well before her mother or sister woke. Rekha was ecstatic, but also scared as well. She was torn between tell Jyoti, so she could share her joy with someone and being horribly disappointed and humiliated, by her mother, who Rekha knew had the power to easily smash her dreams into tiny little pieces. Because she had not had much to be happy about the past few years and nothing to look forward to, except housework. She kept her happiness to herself, patient but fearful, waiting for someone to say something. Waiting for something to happen.

Each time, Bapoojee walked into the kitchen, her heart thumped loudly with anticipation, waiting for him to say something about the wedding. For days he was his normal self and smiled at her, doing his normal chit-chat about this and that. Ba was her usual stony silent self, unless she was complaining about something she didn't like the girls had done or not done in the kitchen or house. For the week,

Rekha was on edge. She was less chatty with Jyoti, who kept asking if something was wrong. Rekha kept rebuffing her with sharp answers, almost barking at her sister. Rekha felt remorseful treating her one and only true friend and confidante so badly. But she was at her wits end and was so on edge, she was cross with everyone in the house, even the baby. Eventually, after a couple of days, Jyoti stopped asking, but still kept a watchful eye on Rekha, suspecting that she had some kind of health issue. She supposed it could be Rekha's monthlies coming, the only thing Jyoti could think would be causing her sister to so irritable with everyone. But with a house of girls who spent every day of their lives together, intimate details of each other's menstrual cycles were not easily hidden. Although each took care of their own used rags, with a good rinse after use, Rekha was the one who took complete responsibility of the laundry, had the task of washing and sanitising the soiled rags the women used regularly.

And then Sunday came, normal in every way, nothing out of the ordinary. They had just finished eating their lunch and the girls were drying the dishes from the meal. The boys had gone out to play with their friends. They would probably arrive in time for supper, covered with dust and dirt, accompanied with huge smiles of contentment from their latest adventure or silly pranks they played on some innocent bystander. Rekha really envied the boys, especially at times like these. *To be free without rules constraining you and eyes watching your every move. To run around the neighbourhood, not having to worry about what people would say. To play with complete abandonment and enjoy the company of other people, laughing and joking about anything and everything. Oh, what a life...to be a boy! In my next life,* Rekha promised herself, *it will happen. I will make it happen! Just watch me, she promised to nobody and everybody.* But no one was watching or cared. Rekha would never voice these sentiments out loud. So, only *Bhagvan* was listening, but he didn't seem to care too much about the plight of any Indian girl right now. *Get back to work, you silly girl*! Rekha heard the voice of her mother in her head, who had not spoken a word. She quickly looked behind to see if her mother had spoken, but there wasn't anyone there. She was at the kitchen table cleaning the crumbs of today's lunch. In the corner of the room, sat her father, who was relaxing on his day off from the shop. He always enjoyed this time, casually gazing through the newspaper, listening to the news on the radio, or some English program that he always listened to. *See, even men, like the Christian God gets a day off! When do I get a day off?* Rekha was brought back to reality as she noticed her mother pick up Lakshmi from her seat, a sturdy box cushioned with old blankets. Lakshmi, at the age of 14 months was still not able to sit up on her own and they had to improvise with different tools to help her sit up. This was especially necessary when they were all busy, doing chores around the house and she had to be put down to keep their hands free. The rest of the time, she sat in someone's arms and had to be carried around. Ba headed to her bedroom to put the baby down for her afternoon nap and but stopped midway.

"Rekha, put some water to boil for *chaa* and, Jyoti, put out some *rusks* and jam tarts out on the table. Your Babookaka and Bhartikaki are coming over to visit in a little while. Also, watch the two little ones while I put Lakshmi down for a sleep," Ba instructed as she walked to her room.

"Jee, Ba," the girls replied in unison, and they finished putting away the lunch dishes to start the next task. The two little ones, Rita and Ramesh were sitting quietly on the sofa. It was Sunday, and everyone took the opportunity of the day off from work to visit. The girls went to work, efficiently as ever. Soon enough, as Rekha put out the cups and saucers for the tea, Babookaki and Bhartikaki walked in and settled themselves At the table and greeted them with big smiles. Bapoojee, put down his newspaper and joined them at the kitchen table. Ba was still in the room. Babookaka went to the little ones and played with them for a few minutes. The girls waited, standing at the table for their mother to come in and sit. They knew better than to make themselves comfortable with the adults unless instructed by their mother to join them.

"Well, this is definitely a happy time for us all now, isn't it?" Bhartikaki beamed with her eyes shining with happiness. She moved toward Rekha to hug her. Rekha startled, took a step back and looked at her with big round eyes, taking a few seconds, although it felt like a few minutes in the silence that seemed to fill the air, to understand what she was saying. Bhartikaki reached out and rubbed her arms in affection.

"Ah, yes, it is," Rekha replied with a small smile. She was not sure how to act. The heart began to thump loudly in her chest. Her mind was swirling with anticipation.

Oh God, it is finally happening! Should I pretend to not know what was about to happen? What else could I do at this point, no one had said a thing to her yet! Maybe, it is something else they are speaking of...maybe Bhartikaki is having a child and that is why they are happy! She quickly stole a glance at Jyoti to see if how she was reacting or even understanding what Bhartikaki was speaking of. Jyoti was smiling politely and nodding at Bhartikaki but when their aunt looked away to smile at Babookaka and the little children, Rekha got the 'look' from her sister. She knew that Jyoti was confused, but she remained being polite to Bhartikak, so not to upset her or anyone. Before Rekha could react to Jyoti, Babookaka walked over to Rekha and gave her a quick hug around the shoulders. Jyoti was increasingly confused and desperately wanted to know what was going on. Rekha knew there was no way she could explain anything to her sister. And she was not completely sure she should say anything at all to Jyoti. So, she was compelled by her own insecurity to remain silent and compliant to the adults around them.

"We are so happy for you and I am sure your parents are also so happy, my girl." He beamed at Rekha and swung around to smile broadly at his brother who had put his newspaper down and sat watching them congratulate Rekha. "Well *Bhai,* let's get down to business and get this started, we don't have too much time now," he urged his brother.

"Yes, you are right about that, let's sit down and get started. Rekha, come and sit down with us for a minute. Your mother will come in a minute. Jyoti... is everything on the table?" he asked.

"Jee, Bapoojee," she confirmed and went silent, still not able to take her eyes off her Rekha.

Just then, their mother walked into the kitchen, stopped to assess the table to see if anything was missing. Satisfied, she sat down next to her sister-in-law, while Rekha's father joined her, in the seat next to her. Rekha, was smiling with joy until her mother walked in. She sat down to join the adults at the table. Rekha's face was solemn and straight, as not to show too much happiness or emotion of any kind. Jyoti went and sat down on the chesterfield, where the little ones played and waited. She was very curious to hear what was going on, but also stayed, in case she was needed to bring anything for the meeting taking place. And neither of her parents had asked her to leave, so she assumed it was alright to stay. Jyoti was extremely curious to understand why Rekha was sitting with the adults. Although she pretended to be preoccupied with the little ones, she was listening to every word being uttered. The children were rarely ever involved in any decision making or planning of the family, so this was not normal. Rekha quickly realised that she was sitting on the side of the table where she was in the line of vision of her mother and her sister, right behind her. Rekha kept her face free of emotion, moving her eyes from her father to Babookaka to Bhartikaki and back again. She was not going to look at her mother and see her angry face. Rekha did not really know if her mother was angry or upset or anything. In fact, her mother's face was quite blank. She willed herself not to look at her, especially at such an important moment like this. By not looking at her mother, she also avoided the gaze of her dear sister who was still wondering about this impromptu meeting. Rekha wanted to remember the faces of people who loved her and cared about her. Rekha did not want to remember the face of the woman who took every opportunity to demean her and humiliate her.

"So, Rekha, your uncle and aunt are here to help us get ready for your *lagan-wedding*. We have set a date and it is coming soon, we only have a few weeks. We have to work fast," Bapoojee stated matter-a-fact. The adults nodded vigorously in agreement.

"Jee Bapoojee, whatever you think is best," Rekha looked at her father nodded. She really wanted to jump up and hug him, but she knew better, she forced herself not to show anything in front of mother. Rekha's eyes flitted to Jyoti for a second, taking the chance that her eyes would cross paths with her mother, but she had to, she could not help it when she saw a small movement in the back of the room. Jyoti's hand had gone to her mouth to smother the loud intake of breath. She was careful not to lock eyes with Jyoti, not wanting to look at her sister for so many reasons. But in split second glance, she saw the tears already flowing down her sister's face. Nobody saw them. Rekha turned away from her sister and kept her gaze on her mug of *chaa*. Both Kaka and Kaki were looking at Rekha smiling, remembering the moment they had told their daughter of her impending wedding and how she, all of them, had been so happy at that time. The smiles, the hugs and tears of joy that filled their house that day. But they saw nothing of that happiness, and stopped smiling and looked at each other, noting the muted tone in the room and the lack of joy, at this typically joyful moment in a young woman's life. They hoped that Rekha was happy with the news, but they did not say anything. This seemed more like business and nothing more. But really, they knew why Rekha was acting this way, and went along with the act, not wanting cause too much trouble and instead support Rekha, in any way they could.

"Your Babookaka was kind enough to speak to the boy's parents this morning. And they are back with news. The boy's family is satisfied with the date that the priest has chosen. It will be on June 10." Bapoojee nodded and smiled in the direction of his brother, showing his gratitude for his assistance, and getting this union confirmed so quickly. Rekha nodded and gave her uncle a quick smile to acknowledge his part in making this happen.

"Go on now Rekha. Help Jyoti put the little ones to sleep for their nap. We have a lot to talk about," Ba said.

"Jee Ba," Rekha answered and got up. Her palms were sweaty, her head spinning while her heart was pounding with joy, she was sure everyone could hear it.

"There is a lot of work, but don't worry, we are here for you all," Bhartikaki assured everyone at the table, "and Rekha we will see you soon," pointing at her niece. Rekha gave her a warm smile in response as she walked to Jyoti and the children. The girls took the littles ones to their room. One sister with huge smile, the other sister forcing the tears back.

Both brothers understood the necessity of expediting this marriage, in fact, everyone except Jyoti, understood the reason for the rushed plans. Although no one spoke of it, it was there, hanging in the room, like a dark cloud. They understood that this marriage had to happen and be soon to keep the gossip-mongers quiet, while also maintaining their integrity and honour in the small community of Boksburg, Johannesburg, and the larger community of Indians in their new home country. The parents at the table understood they needed this community, good and bad, today and tomorrow to survive, to keep their way of life, culture and religion intact. They needed the community for their business to thrive, they needed the community for support in the good times and the bad times. So, for the sake of their children and their children's children, their family would survive this and anything else that came their way. They had to get this done as quickly as possible. They did not have time for a grand affair, as they had begun with Manjuben's wedding. Out of respect for the family's loss, Rekha's parents agreed that this wedding would be understated. But Rekha did not know this.

Chapter 18

The adults continued their plans for the wedding preparations, which went well into the night, as the girls got their younger siblings ready for bed after a quick meal. The older boys came in later and settled themselves in for the night. Tomorrow was Monday, and the weekly schedule would begin for them all. Rekha and Jyoti were also in bed, but awake, with Rita fast asleep between them. She slept with her arms above her head and legs splayed over her sisters, trying to cover as space as she could in the bed. The girls laid in bed, wide awake, both staring at the ceiling, lost in their own thoughts, both not knowing how to break the silence hanging over them. Jyoti did not say much as they prepared for bed. She was very quiet, unlike her usual bedtime routine, when the two of them would chatter and giggle until their heads hit their pillows. But not this night. This night, both girls were lost in their own thoughts and Rekha did not even notice Jyoti's quietness. This night, Jyoti's heart was broken and Rekha's heart thumped wildly in her chest, excited to finally hear about the wedding date. She had wanted to jump and down with happiness when her father gave the date, but she was scared her mother would slap her for not behaving. She had wanted to hug Bhartikaki and Babookaki and soak in the love and affection they wanted to give. But she had held herself together, quiet, and tightly wound, not to show too much emotion. Mixed in with excitement, she felt relief. No more hiding and pretending that she knew this was coming. *It is finally going to happen! The years of waiting had been close to unbearable. I am going to be married! And I am going to get away from here…away from her!*

"Rekha…are you still awake?" Jyoti whispered to her sister. *Oh, no, I forgot about Jyoti.* Rekha closed her eyes, dreading the questions coming her way. She could tell from the smallness of her voice, she was sad. The girls knew that tonight, suddenly, there seemed to be a large widening gap between them. As every second passed the gap grew bigger and bigger. Jyoti had noticed small changes in her sister for a few days now. Rekha had become more terse, more impatient with all of the siblings, especially Jyoti. The two sisters stopped chatting at night like they used to. Recently, it had been Jyoti doing all the talking and Rekha just giving the occasional brief answer. Jyoti did not know how to bring up this new bad behaviour, afraid of Rekha's new sharp tongue. Jyoti did not recognise this person anymore. Rekha was always nice to Jyoti, no matter what happened, even when Ba was horrible. Jyoti was more careful about the way she spoke to her sister and tried to avoid any confrontation. Of course, Rekha had been so swept up in her happiness, all this time and especially now, not seeing that she had become this different person. She was so focused and determined to be free and happy, that she had not thought about anyone else, even Jyoti. At least two hours had passed since Rekha had been told the announcement of the wedding and the girls had not yet talked. Rekha had already forgotten about the tears her sister had shed earlier, when their father had broken the news. She was so wrapped in her own joy; she did not give anyone else a thought. Even her much beloved Manjuben was forgotten in this moment, whose death was the very reason this wedding was taking place so soon. Rekha would not realise this until much later, what affect Manjuben's death would have on the rest of her life. She did not want to think about anything else, except her new life.

"Yes, I am," Rekha finally answered, trying not to show too much happiness in voice. She did not want to hurt her sister more than she was hurt already.

"Did you know?" she asked.

"What!? Why would you say that? How could I know?" Rekha challenged in a hiss.

"Well, it is just that when Bapoojee told you about the wedding date, you…" Jyoti hesitated, and Rekha jumped in.

"What? I what?" Rekha countered with irritation, lifting her head and looking straight at her sister, not realising her voice had risen in the dark room. Rita, between the two sisters, sighed in her sleep and squirmed, made Rekha quiet down immediately and also remembering the adults were still in the kitchen. She could still hear them faintly, and she was more concerned that they would hear her then upsetting Jyoti or waking the little one. Jyoti turned in the bed, her back to Rekha, not wanting to look at her sister's face. She knew that Rekha was agitated, perhaps from this announcement, or perhaps from something else, she couldn't think clearly, it was all too much to think about right now. She did not want to push Rekha or upset her, but

Jyoti was feeling hurt and afraid needed to know. She spoke calmly and slowly.

"Well, maybe I am wrong and maybe I am right, but you didn't look surprised at all," Jyoti stated with a resigned note. "I was wondering why? Why weren't you surprised?"

"Don't be silly!" Rekha countered without answering the question.

"And even now, you have not said one word to me about the wedding plans. Are you not happy about this?"

Rekha took her time replying to her sister. She was flustered, unsure how to respond. At that moment, Rekha decided not to tell Jyoti the truth, not quite sure herself why she would choose to lie to her sister, her one and only confidante. She knew that she had gone too far, since the time she had omitted the truth after overhearing her parents. She was determined to follow through with her deception. *She had no idea that I knew already. Nobody knows that I knew. I can just pretend like before. There was no need to be angry with her. I am going to have a wonderful life. I should be kinder to her.*

Taking a deep breath, Rekha calmed herself and answered in an even tone.

"Look, I was surprised. I really was," she lied to her sister, using the softest tone she could muster and continued, "and it was just a shock, and it took me a while to understand it all. And…and she was sitting in front of me and watching me. I didn't want her to see. To see, how happy I really was."

"Oh," Jyoti responded quietly. She understood now, not much explanation was needed. But Jyoti's heart was still sore, thinking how in a few months' time, she would alone and unhappy without her big sister. No one to talk to. No one to laugh and giggle with. Her one and only true friend in this world would be leaving her. Jyoti's weak response irritated Rekha to no end. *She was clearly not happy for me. She, of all people, should understand how desperate I am to leave this house and have a happy life. I deserve a happy life.*

"How do you think I should have acted? Should I have jumped and clapped my hands and sing a happy song!?" Rekha asked snidely, while still keeping her voice down. Rekha was still very aware that her parents and uncle and aunt were in the kitchen.

"No. You were right not to overreact. Ba would have been very cross. She would have *given it* to you later," Jyoti conceded. The room went silent as they both contemplated the various scenarios of how Ba acted when she was unhappy about something. Sometimes, it would have nothing to do with something the girls had done. Anything could set her off. The babies crying too much, the food not tasting right, taking too long to bring something for her and especially if the girls did not clean the house to her standards.

"But it is very soon, isn't?" Jyoti finally asked quietly.

"Not soon enough for me," Rekha replied with complete selfishness and coldness in her heart, "I would leave tomorrow if I had the chance."

"Well, maybe all that praying and fasting finally worked," Jyoti offered.

"Yes, you are probably right, *Bhagvan* has finally answered my prayers," Rekha confirmed, knowing all too well, that God and prayers, had nothing to do with her upcoming wedding. She did not deny Jyoti's comment, not wanting to her sister to lose her faith. It also helped Rekha with completing the deception she had created, which had gone too far for any truth revelation. Rekha saw no need to change any part of the story. Rekha was being selfish, but not realising or caring that she was. At this time, she felt no compulsion to reveal the truth. She understood that the truth served no purpose for her or anyone else.

"I really hope you get everything you deserve," Jyoti uttered with a choke, wiping her eyes in the dark. As if she could hide her unhappiness from her sister. Jyoti meant it; she sincerely wanted the best for her sister. But that did not stop Jyoti from feeling a little sorry for herself. She felt that she had already lost a bit of her sister tonight. Although she was lying in bed with Rekha and Rita, she felt alone and afraid.

"We must really get some sleep, we have some work to do," Rekha reminded Jyoti, completely ignoring Jyoti's last statement. Rekha suddenly felt uneasy, hearing how much her sister cared about her. She waited for Jyoti to say something else, but Jyoti had turned over with her back to her sister and waited for the pull of sleep to come to her. Within minutes, Jyoti was fast asleep, tired from the emotional shock of this evening's announcement and her sister's emotional withdrawal from her. She let sleep do its job, releasing her from anguish of it all. Rekha, waited and heard nothing and finally relaxed a little. She had felt quick pang of guilt, but it was very brief, and the selfishness came back quick and strong. *Oh please stop talking and go to sleep! Why are you making this so difficult for me? I will get everything I deserve. I have worked like a dog all these years and I promised myself I would have a better life. I am ready now. I just have to be patient for only a few months now.* Rekha did not really know what was in store for her. She could only hope that anything was better than this life she had now. A husband who would treat her right. She really had no concept of what love really was and what it could be. She had no understanding of what adults did behind closed doors. It was never discussed or explained. All she knew was that, you needed a husband to have babies and there was physical intimacy involved. A lot of touching and kissing would happen. Her understanding of marriage was from what she saw in her parent's marriage and her Kaka and Kaki's marriage – having a person in her life who could provide a house, clothes and food for herself and her children. She still did not understand that a person, a man – her husband, even as a married woman, would have complete control. *All she saw was the promise of freedom.*

Chapter 19

The days and weeks moved much faster than anyone had anticipated, everyone was very busy getting things ready for the wedding. The wedding was only a few days away now. It was almost of a repeat of what they had to do for Manjuben's wedding, with many shortcuts and leaving out of many parts. Everyone had their moments of tiredness and tension, especially the parents of both families. Jyoti, slowly withdrew from her sister and spent less time with her and only when it was required in the kitchen. With the wedding plans in full swing, she spent most of her time looking after the children, while Rekha continued with her chores in the kitchen and with laundry. All free moments were spent getting ready for the wedding. Just like with Manjuben's wedding, although Rekha took very time to consider Manjuben anymore, she was too busy. The clothes for the children had to be made, the suits for the boys had to measured and bought. The house had to be repaired and cleaned. Items for all meals before and during the wedding had to be ordered, stored, ready for preparations. Everyone would go to their beds, exhausted from the pace they kept up, everyone except Rekha, who was tireless and filled with eternal spark of fiery energy. She was moving, constantly moving, going around the clock from the moment she opened her eyes in the morning, until she put her head down on the pillow at night. She did whatever her mother bid her do and she did it quickly and efficiently. She was fired up from within, consumed with the hope of tomorrow. Jyoti saw it and felt but did not dare say anything. Rekha was not very chatty these days. She was busy and determined to get things done. They had to be done so she could get married. Jyoti learned to be patient and not to ask too many questions, lest she received the bite of Rekha's impatience during her preoccupation with the wedding. Jyoti remained quiet and did what she was expected to do. She watched her sister and wondered where the new energy came from? She was not happy or serene like Manjuben had been. Instead, her sister was doing things and doing it with purpose. Rekha was always moving around the house, doing this and that. But no one was included or consulted. Rekha was locked away in her own little world. Her own world of a wedding, marriage, and a husband. A world that Jyoti would not know for a long while. Jyoti did not know that Rekha's thoughts were filled with her new life. That was what gave such energy and strength. Every chore Rekha completed now, was considered in a new light. *When I am married, I will cook for this my husband...When I am married, I will wash and iron his shirts...When I am married, I will wear nice clothes. When I am married, I will have a maid to clean the house...When I am married, I will play with my child and I will be happy.*

On the Wednesday before the wedding day, Rekha finished chores quickly because earlier in the morning, when she was cleaning the dishes from the Breakfast, Babookaka came in from the shop. He grabbed a cup of tea and some jam biscuits. He stood next to her, by the sink and spoke to her, while slurping the tea and munching on as many biscuits as he could.

"When you are finished with your work, your Kaki and I would like you to spend one last night with us. And don't worry my girl," seeing Rekha's furrowed brow, "I have already spoken to your mother and father and they are fine with it." He gave a huge smile and a wink, as he grabbed two more biscuits.

"Jee Babookaka," she smiled back at him, looked quickly around to see if her mother was around and listening, "I would like that too. I will finish my work quickly today."

"That is fine, I will see you at home then."

Rekha was so happy and grinned at her uncle as he walked away, looking forward to an evening with her uncle and aunt. Later that afternoon, while she was getting her clothes for the night's stay, her heart sunk a little with a sadness. She realised that this night would the last night she would ever sleep in Babookaka's and Bhartikaki's house. She finished packing her night bag and let her mother and sister know that she was going and quickly left. She still feared that she would be called back because her mother had found another chore for her to do. She walked swiftly as she could, to get away and to get in as much time as she could with her favourite uncle and aunt. The thought of losing them, brought tears to her eyes. *I will never do this again*, she thought, *I will never be able to enjoy their company in their home ever again. This is the last time. Oh Manjuben, I wish you were here! I miss you.* Rekha's feet moved faster and faster as her mind filled with all the things she would miss. Her uncle, her aunt, her younger siblings and the two people she had completely forgotten about, her father and her sister – Jyoti. *Oh no, what will I do without them!? What will they do without me?* Rekha had been so wrapped in her own happiness, she had forgotten who she was leaving behind. As she approached their door, she shook her head to shake off the sadness threatening to overwhelm her. She stood outside for a few seconds, taking in the moment, and forcing a smile on her face. Rekha wanted this last visit to be a happy one for all of them. She opened the door and walked in.

"Oh, there you are," Bhartikaki greeted from across the kitchen, "I was hoping you would come earlier. I have the tea ready and all your favourites. Come, sit my girl." she said, placing plates of *rusks*, *gulab jamun*, jam tarts and *chevro* on the table. Bhartikaki had taken out her china set usually reserved for guests. Everything was beautifully set out for the two of them.

"There is so much food here Kaki, I can't eat all of this!"

"Don't worry, you don't have to eat it all. I just wanted to have everything that you like. And besides, I am sure your Kaka and cousins will help you finish it when they come home," she assured Rekha with a laugh. They sat and enjoyed their tea and snacks for a good hour just chatting and laughing.

"Everything is ready for Sunday? Your mother must be so frantic with all the things she has to remember," Kaki asked in concern, remembering how stressed she had been preparing for Manjuben's wedding.

"No, she is fine. Jyoti and I have been helping her and everything should be ready."

"Good, I am glad that. You know, this morning, I was thinking about your sister."

"My sister? Why?" Rekha asked in confusion.

"Well, she is probably very sad that you are leaving house. She is going miss you so much. I know how close you two are," Bharti commented in sympathy.

"Oh," Rekha replied softly. She didn't know what to say and was suddenly ashamed that she had not given Jyoti much thought since the announcement of her wedding. Her mouth went dry and she swallowed the lump of guilt that lodged in her throat. Bhartikaki mistook her silence for sadness, having to leave her sister. She tried to reassure Rekha in the best way she could.

"Don't worry, my girl, I will keep an eye out for her. That poor thing will be so busy looking after the children and taking over your chores as well," Bhartikaki commented searching Rekha's face for some response, but she received none, so she didn't push the discussion anymore. Feeling sorry for the two sisters at being separated.

"Come Rekha. I want to show you something." Bhartikaki got up from the table, with a smile, walking toward the bedrooms.

"Kaki, I will come. Let me just wash the cups and saucers," Rekha said.

"No, leave it. The dishes can wait," Bhartikaki said.

"Alright," Rekha agreed and got up to join Kaki, she still looked at the table and the dishes, feeling guilty that she was walking away and leaving the mess. She followed Bhartikaki to the bedroom. Her aunt went to the corner of the room and removed a blanket that covered something. Rekha moved closer and couldn't believe her eyes.

"You remember this? I am sure Manju must have shown it to you," Bhartiaki asked, but really not expecting an answer from Rekha. She saw the answer on Rekha's face.

"I want you, my sweet girl, to have it."

"What? No, no. I can't take it. It belongs to Manjuben." Rekha shook her head with surprise, unable to stop her hand from touching the trousseau box that Manjuben had shown her. Rekha remembered how happy and proud Manjuben had been, showing her all the beautiful items of clothing in the iron chest.

"Now, please…your Kaka and I discussed it and agreed that you should have it. We don't have any girls to give this to. We want you to have it. Please say yes," she pleaded with tears in her eyes. Rekha looked at Bhartikaki and saw the deep hurt that her aunt tried so hard to hide from everyone. Bhartikaki pulled Rekha into a long embrace. Both of them crying over the loss of Manjuben and now Bhartikaki and Rekha were losing each other.

"Promise me that you will make use of these things. And when you wear them, you remember my beautiful Manju. You will remember me and your Kaka, because we will be thinking about you." Bhartikaki wiped the tears from her face with end of her sari and then wiped the tears from Rekha's face, who hid her face in her Kaki's shoulder. They stood together, crying and hugging for a while. Bhartikaki had later told Rekha that this had been discussed with her parents, since there was very little time to do the typical wedding shopping. There had been no issue on either side of this decision.

Later, Babookaka found them both still in the room, with all the clothes admiring all the beautiful colours and material. He stood at the door of the room, holding a cup of tea and *gulab jamun* in his hand.

"I came as soon as I could, the shop was so busy today," he mumbled through the food in his mouth. Rekha, rushed to her uncle and grabbed his middle, hugging him hard.

"Thank you Babookaka. Thank you so much," she whispered with catch in her voice, speaking to his chest, unable to look at her uncle.

"No, my dear. Thank you," he answered with a solemn face, balancing his tea and biscuit, desperately trying not to spill, "you have been so good to us. We want you to be happy."

That evening, everyone went to bed with unhappy hearts. Rekha in Manjuben's bed for the last time, tossing and turning. Her mind filled with memories of Manjuben and the guilt that she would not spend anymore nights with her uncle and aunt. What made her feel the worst was the guilt about abandoning Jyoti. Bhartikaki had put it in bluntly enough that Jyoti would be responsible for everything. And she would be alone. There would nobody there to chat with, laugh with, cry with…she would alone with Ba! *Oh, my poor Jyoti! I have been so selfish, not giving her a single thought about how her life would be.*

But what can I do about that? Rekha wracked her brain, thinking of ways to help her sister came to the final answer. She could do nothing at all for Jyoti. There were no choices or exits for women, except the ones offered to them. *I will be married and living in another house. I can do nothing. She will have to endure and wait, just like I did.* She resigned herself to the inability to change anything or anyone. Rekha finally turned over and forced herself to sleep, she had so much to do with only a few days left.

Chapter 20

Sunday finally came…it was still dark, the sun had not risen but Rekha, Jyoti and her parents were up, each taking their turn to bathe. The boys and little ones bathed later. The girls made the breakfast for everyone as usual. They took out all the tins and containers full of sweets and savouries to serve the guests. It was decided for the sake of time and money and not to be ostentatious, they would only serve tea and savouries, not lunch as was customary. All the items for the *Brahmin*, priest, was accounted for and kept together under the watchful eye of Ba. Bapoojee held the envelope, payment for the *Brahmin's* services, in his suit blazer pocket. The priest had been given strict instructions to do the fastest version he could, with just the fire and exchange of garlands and be finished and done. These ceremonies, plus the bride and groom were the most important things needed for the wedding to happen.

Bhartikaki had arrived with her boys, all of them already dressed for the wedding. Babookaka had gone to the hall to make sure all everything was ready. Bapoojee, fresh out of the shower and half dressed with just his trousers and long sleeves shirt, came out to have some breakfast. Everyone grabbed a seat, when they could, after the girls set the *bekkers* of tea on the table with some buttered toast and rusks. Ba gave the youngest her milk, while the girls and Bhartikaki fed the little ones. Everyone stuffed themselves, knowing that it would a busy day for all of them and they would not get a chance to eat at their leisure. Only Rekha did not eat, she was fasting for the wedding having only some fruit and warm milk, with crushed almonds. It would keep her going for most of the day until she was allowed to eat after the wedding ceremony. The wedding time was set for 10 am at the hall and the sun was rising, as the girls washed the dishes and cleared up the breakfast food and put it all away. There was scurry of people getting up from the kitchen table. They realised it was time for everyone to get dressed and be on their way. Bhartikaki went in the room with the girls and helped Rekha get dressed. Bhartikaki had sent over the trousseau over the next day after Rekha had slept over. From Manjuben's, now Rekha's trousseau, Ba, Bhartikaki and Rekha had picked a soft cotton *sari*, dusky white with a slight hint of rose pink that ran along the border hem for Rekha to wear for the wedding. It was soft, unique and understated. After the trunk had been delivered, Rekha, Jyoti and Ba went through the trunk and made sure some of the plain sari blouses had been adjusted to fit Rekha. It was expected that Rekha would be wearing saris from now on as a married woman, especially in her in-laws' house, and they had to be simple to do the housework. Manjuben was tall and thin with narrow shoulders. Luckily there was ample material inside of each blouse, that could be taken out for Rekha's broader shoulders and larger bosom. Rekha would have to adjust the remainder of the blouses, when she had time in her husband's house. For the last few days, there had been very little discussion between the two sisters. They both had been too busy with the children, household chores and preparations for the wedding. Jyoti was withdrawn and did not say much to Rekha unless it had to do with the house or the children. Jyoti wore the dress that Rekha was going to wear for Manjuben's wedding. It also had to be adjusted to fit Jyoti's smaller frame. The older boys – Jayesh and Arun – and the two boy cousins all wore the same outfit, new dark grey suits with white shirts and dark grey ties. Rita was dressed in a pink dress with frills on the collar and a ruffled skirt. She had on a pair of white laced socks and new black buckled shoes. She was very pleased with her first fancy outfit, spinning to watch her twirling skirt. Ba and Bhartikaki wore similar shades of lavender in silk, with slight variations in the pattern of the sari border. They both looked very beautiful with the hair wound up in tight buns, wearing their best gold earrings, bangles and necklace. Ramesh, also in his first fancy outfit, had long trousers, with a white shirt and dark grey vest with a black bow tie.

Bapoojee was seated at the kitchen, dressed in his finest suit, patiently waiting for the women to get ready. The boys were outside with Bapoojee's car and a neighbour who had borrowed a car for the day. Finally, Rekha emerged from the hallway and into the kitchen for the last time. Rekha would be going directly to her in-laws' house after the wedding. Her father got up, beaming at his first-born.

"You are ready, I see, my *dikri*," he said as she walked toward him. Rekha was shy, all of the sudden, unable to meet her father's gaze. She had never felt this way before with her father.

"You look very nice for your husband." He patted her cheek gently, taking in her new appearance, with her sari, makeup and jewellery.

"Thank you Bapoojee," Rekha simply answered, with her eyes down, still at a loss for words. Her hair was perfumed and oiled, parted in the middle, with a long braid down her back reaching past her waist. She had small pearl earrings on her ears, with two matching gold bangles with pearls on each forearm, also filled with smaller glass white bangles. These were all items borrowed from Manjuben's trousseau, but nobody made mention of it. It didn't matter to Rekha or anyone else. Today, was Rekha's day and it seemed all of it had been bought and made for her. Her head was covered with the sari, as was the custom for bride, with some tiny pink flowers down the braid, barely visible beneath her thin material of her *sari*. She had a light shade of pink lipstick on, and her eyes were bold and vibrant lined with *kohl*. She had a light dusting of face powder, but the flush of her cheeks stood out, looking like she was wearing blush. Until today, Rekha had never worn any makeup, except for the *kohl,* before this and it felt strange to her, saying nothing as her Bhartikaki had taken meticulous care applying it for her. Jyoti noticed that she did not look like a girl, but rather a woman, a beautiful woman, ready to become a wife. And it seemed that way to everyone, finally giving her the respect and honour as was expected to be given, to any married woman. Ba did not have a single bad word to say all week. Even now, she fussed over Rekha's hair and *sari*, patting here and there and tugging the *sari* to make sure everything was in its place. Rekha was uneasy with this attention, especially from her mother, but kept still and quiet, knowing there would never be another moment like between her mother and herself.

"Come, let us go. The hall will be filling up with people now and we should not be late," Bapoojee instructed everyone. He gave them all a smile of approval as they walked out of the house. Jyoti took care of Rita, Bhartikaki had Ramesh and Ba had Lakshmi. There were two cars ready to take them all to the hall, one was the family's car, and the other car was borrowed from a neighbour, driven by Babookaka himself. He had returned from the hall and decorated the borrowed car with flowers and ribbons, on the door handles and front bonnet. Everyone was impressed with his efforts, the boys were whistled and winked at Babookaka, who revelled in the attention. He was overwhelmed with pride when he saw a beautiful young woman Rekha, in her elegant *sari*. He saw a vision of loveliness, very mature and beautiful, with her head down, a small garland of flowers around her neck, the traditionally decorated coconut held in both hands. While he admired her, she was shocked and happy to see the fancy car and her mouth dropped open, as she took in the shiny, decorated Ford sedan. She couldn't believe that he had gone to all this trouble for her. She gave her uncle a big grin, forgetting her that she was to be the shy, quiet, unassuming bride for today.

"Well, looking very *lekker* today, my girl!" Babookaki smiled back, snapping his fingers and giving her an appreciative whistle. Rekha's head was swimming with all this attention and excitement. *So many compliments! I must look very nice!? But what will the bridegroom, my husband, think of me? It has so long since I last saw him...I wonder what he will look now?*

"That Bharat Lala is going to very happy today," Babokaki offered, as if reading her mind. Both Rekha and Jyoti smothered giggles, as their mother shook her head and gave Babookaka a grimace in response. He took no offense, giving the girls, seated in the back, a wink as he helped Ba into the front with Lakshmi. More giggles erupted from Rekha and Jyoti, quickly covering their mouths, as their mother turned around with a stern look. The cars were packed with all the necessary items for the Brahmin and the wedding. Rekha's trousseau, loaded in Bapoojee's car, was also packed in one *peti*, a metal traveling trunk, with a few articles of her own clothing were already packed in the trunk of the borrowed car. They all piled into the two cars, the girls being especially careful with their dresses and saris, as they were seated in the wedding car. Bapoojee took all the boys in his car, including Ramesh who was thoroughly enjoying an outing with his brothers, bouncing on back seat. Rekha seated herself between Bhartikaki and Jyoti, who had Rita on her lap. All the women had sat in the official wedding car, smiling and waving as people honked, seeing the wedding decorations. It was the latest model of the cream-coloured Ford Sedan, quite expensive and handsome, with its flashy chrome trimmings and upholstered seats and linings. Babookaki playfully honked the horn and it became a game all the way to the hall. Rekha and Jyoti thoroughly enjoyed the ride, very pleased with themselves and the attention they received from total strangers. Some of the waving strangers were actually white people! She and Jyoti forgot about the wedding, waving and laughing with happiness at the joyous raucous their car was creating. Even little Rita was waving and jumping up and down in Jyoti's lap. But what seemed like just minutes, they had arrived at the hall. Ba saw the crowd standing outside the hall and quickly turned in her seat and gave Jyoti and Rekha a stern look, basically indicating they had to stop their giggling and stop smiling. This was supposed to be a solemn occasion, when the bride leaves her family. This was not a time for laughing, giggling and having a good time. The ladies in the crowd jostled and craned their head to get a look at Rekha. They wanted to see what she was wearing on every part of her body, up close, so they could have the opportunity to admire or criticize the bride and her choices. Ba, Bhartikaki and Babookaka took control of the bridal party and rushed Rekha into the hall quickly, giving people as little to talk about as possible.

As soon the car had arrived at the hall, Rekha suddenly felt a twinge of panic and fright. She tried to avert the eyes of the people in the crowd, by keeping her head down, luckily the sari on her head offered enough protection from the inquisitive eyes. *My God, there are so many people here! How many people did Ba and Bapoojee invite?* She took in the scene, as best she could from her veiled face. She would not get a chance to see or notice anything very soon. The hall was filled and there was a steady drone of conversation, accompanied or in competition of the wedding music being played on cassette tape with large speakers. In the middle of the hall, with chairs set up around it, was the wedding *mandap – a canopied altar with pillars.* It was simple, nothing too extravagant or flashy. In the first rows of chairs, sat the women guests, with their children, sisters, mothers, sisters-in-law and mothers-in-law. The men and young men of the families, stood at the back of the hall, holding up the walls, standing in their small little groups, puffing away on cigarettes, trying to look dashing and aloof to the surrounding event. Some of the younger boys played between the seating and the wall of men. This way, someone could keep a watchful eye for the little ones, in case of a mishap or bad behaviour. Rekha was guided to sit on a small stool in the *mandap*. She suddenly felt a warm body next to her. *It was him! Bharat was here already, in the hall, in the mandap the whole time. This is really happening!!* The blood rushed out of her head, making her a little dizzy, making her lose control of any logical thought, incapable of moving or saying anything, frozen in fear and excitement. She had no idea what to do, no one had told her or prepared her. She knew that her parents and family sat nearby, but she could not see or hear them. Her palms became sweaty, and her hands shook slightly. Then, she saw feet, next to her, with white socks and a pair of bent bony knees outlined from black trousers. Her head began to spin and she couldn't hear the crowd or the music anymore. The *Brahmin* began the ceremony, lighting the fire, chanting the sacred Sanskrit verses. Rekha's tried to listen to what he was saying but the chatting crowd, in unison with the wedding music made it difficult. She completed the actions asked of her by the priest, but most of the time, she mimicked what Bharat was doing, hoping in vain that was what she was supposed to do as well. The ceremony went quickly, as planned and many people, as they usually did at Indian weddings, walked and talked, losing interest in the ceremony occurring in front to them. They had anticipated a long-drawn-out morning, but it was almost over. The garlands had been exchanged and now it was time for the bride and groom to walk around the sacred fire with seven steps together, holding hands. By holding the bride's hand, the groom accepts her responsibilities and taken the final step to marriage and the beginning of their spiritual union before God and witnesses. Rekha's mind had become numb and she saw and heard nothing. It was happening too quickly and everything was a blur. Bharat, stood in front of Rekha, much taller than she remembered, gently moved back the sari veil from her face, so he could place a red *chandla* – the vermillion mark along Rekha's parted hair on her forehead. She still could not bring herself to look at him fully in the face. She saw a black tie and a clip that held the tie to the white shirt *her husband* was wearing. She felt his hands go around her neck, underneath the *sari* linking a thin chain with gold and black beads, the *Mangal Sutra*, a sign of a married woman. She shivered inside and closed her eyes in the pleasure of his touch. *My husband! I am finally married!*

Rekha took a deep breath and felt someone pressing a handkerchief on her cheeks and under her eyes. *I must be sweating; my makeup must be smearing…*She vaguely thought to herself and opened her eyes. Why else would someone be wiping my face…She took a moment to clear the blurry view in front of her and saw the hand and then the face. It was her mother's hand which held the handkerchief. There she stood, in front of Rekha, gently patting the tears from her daughter's face, not bothering to wipe the tears that flowed down her own face.

"Don't cry my *dikri*, you are married now. Be happy," Ba says quietly with a smile.

Rekha looked at her mother with wet eyes and let out a soft cry, never imagining this moment would ever come. The moment she had hoped for – a new life and a new tomorrow. *I have done it. I am finally free! All her hopes and promises for tomorrow were finally here!*

"Ba!" Rekha cried out, as she looked at her mother's face. She was inconsolable as she said goodbye to her whole family, one by one. She was finally led out of the hall by her husband, still crying, into the car waiting for them to begin their lives as husband and wife.

Glossary

Arti – Indian Hindu religious ritual of worship, a part of puja/prayer, in which light/flame/diva is offered to one or more deities Arti(s) also refers to the songs sung in praise of the deity, when the light is being offered

Bhagavan/Bhagvan – Indian Hindu word to denote God/Lord or anyone who possesses divine qualities

Brahmin – a Hindu person of the highest social rank/also refers to the priest to perform religious rites and prayers

Broekie – Afrikaner/South African slang word meaning panties or ladies underwear

Cha – Indian word for tea, served with milk and sugar

Chai – Indian beverage made with boiled tea leaves, steamed/boiled milk, sweet spices – cardamom, ginger, nutmeg and/or lemongrass and sugar

Chandla – Indian Gujrati word for red dot/powder worn by Hindu women, especially a red-colored one, serves as an auspicious sign of marriage

Chappal – footwear, sandals, similar to a flip-flop with a toe strap

Chevro – Indian snack/part of nastoo consisting of a mixture of spicy, dried ingredients, which may include fried lentils, peanuts, vegetable oil, chickpeas, flaked rice or rice crispies, curry leaves and sometimes even crumbled cornflakes! This is all flavored with salt and a blend of spices

Diva – Indian word for a small lamp made from cotton ball and ghee/clarified butter, used to perform daily puja/prayers and during festivals

Ganesh Puja – a ceremony is held at both the bride and the groom's houses. The bride and the groom along with their respective families offer their prayers to Lord Ganesha to seek his blessings and pray to him to remove all the obstacles coming in their way

Gulab Jamun – Indian dessert/South African version-log shaped donuts made with condensed milk, semolina, fried and dipped in syrup and coated with desiccated coconut flakes

Howzit – South African slang/greeting, often used for "hello"

Kafee – Afrikaans, café, local coffee-house

Khari/Kharo – Indian Gujrati word used to describe having dark pigmentation or being dark or black

Khol/Kajal – is an ancient eye cosmetic, traditionally made by grinding stibnite or charcoal, similar purposes to charcoal used in mascara

Koeksiester – a Afrikaner confectionery made of fried dough infused in syrup or honey, which is a fried ball of dough that is rolled in desiccated coconut. The name derives from the Dutch word "koek", which generally means a wheat flour confectionery.

Kunkoo – red powder (also known as vermillion) made from saffron and turmeric. It is traditionally worn by married Hindu women on the forehead and also used for blessings for religious ceremonies

Lagan – Indian Gujrati word for wedding and marriage

Lekker – South African slang to mean, nice, delicious, good-looking, tasty

Mandhir – Indian temple in Hindu or Jain religion

Mangal Sutra – a gold and black beaded necklace with a gold pendant, placed on the neck of the bride by the bridegroom, signifying the eternal bond and union as wife and husband as part of the wedding ceremony

Mantra – mantra is a sacred utterance, a numinous sound, a syllable, word of phonemes, or a group of words in the Sanskrit

Monthlys – local term used to refer to monthly menstruation flow or period

Naan Katai – Indian eggless sweet cookie made with ghee, gram flour, sugar and cardamom

Nappy/ies – British term for a piece of absorbent material wrapped around a baby's bottom and between its legs to absorb and retain urine and feces; a diaper

Nastoo – Indian word for breakfast, snack or refreshment

Pani – Indian word for water, traditionally served to visitors upon their arrival to the house

Piti/Pithi – Gujarati name for the haldi/turmeric ceremony. In this ceremony, the bride sits on a stool, and the ladies of her family apply a paste of sandalwood, turmeric, rosewater and perfume on her body

Poppet – a British term, endearingly sweet or pretty child or young girl (often used as an affectionate form of address)

Roti – Indian flat round bread, rolled with a velan and cooked on the griddle/teva

Rusks – South African/Afrikaner dry and crunchy cookie, eaten for breakfast or with dipped in tea, similar to the Italian biscotti

Sangeet – an evening of music, song and dance with dandiya (dancing sticks) before the wedding, attended by both families of bride and bridegroom

Shiva/Ganesh/Krishna – some of the many gods of the Hindu pantheon, worshipped for various purposes and ceremonies, at funerals, pujas and weddings

Stoep – Afrikaner word for a terraced porch or entranceway area at front of the door

Tot/Dop – Afrikaner word for small amount or drink of alcohol

Velan – Indian, thin wooden rolling pin used for making roti/chapati and Indian breads

Zam-Buk – British/South African product used for over 100 years, this traditional antiseptic ointment has been soothing cuts, sores, bruises, burns, rashes, insect bites, chapped skin, blisters and much more, made from oil of eucalyptus, camphor oil and thyme oil of sassafras

In Gujarati culture family relations:

These are the "titles" for family members. With the exception of Father, Mother, and Grandparents (who are called by the title only), all of these titles are added after the name of the person.

Father: Pappa, Papa, Bapoojee
Mother: Ba, Ma
Brother (also male cousins): Bhai (e.g., Haresh Bhai)
Brother's Wife: Bhabhi (e.g., Komal Bhabhi)
Sister (also female cousins): Bhen/Ben
Older Sister: Didi/Ben (e.g., Mayuri Didi)
Father's Younger Brother or Father's Younger Cousins (1st, 2nd, 3rd, etc): Kaka or (e.g., Rajesh Kaka)
Father's Younger Brother's Wife: Kaki (e.g., Komal Kaki)
Sister-in-law – Bhabi
Mother's Sister: Masi (e.g., Sneha Masi)
Mother's Sister's Husband: Masa (e.g., Gopal Masa)
Cousins are considered to be "brother" or "sister". Elder cousins' name followed by Bhai or Bhen
Son: Babo, Chokro, Dikro, Lalo
Daughter: Baby, Chokri, Dikri, Lali

Poona Family

Mr. Poona – Bapoojee, Rekha's father

Mrs. Poona – Ba, Rekha's mother

Baboo Poona/Babookaka – younger brother of Rekha's father

Bharti Poona/Bhartikaki – wife of Babookaka, mother of Manju

Manju – eldest daughter of Babookaka and Bhartikaki, 1st cousin to Rekha (Manjuben)

Naresh – Manju's younger twin brother, 12 years old

Haresh – Manju's younger twin brother, 12 years old

Rekha – eldest child/daughter of Mr. and Mrs. Poona, 12 years old

Jayesh – eldest son, second child, 11 years old

Arun – third child, second son 10 years old

Jyoti – second daughter, third 4th child, 9 years old

Ramesh – third son, born when Rekha is 13 years old

Lakshmi – third daughter, born when Rekha is 15 years old
Rita – fifth child and daughter – 9 months old

Lala Family

Mr. Lala – Rekha's future father-in-law

Mrs. Lala – Rekha's future mother-in-law

Bharat – eldest son of Mr. and Mrs. Lala, Rekha's fiancé and husband-to-be